SHERLOCK HOLMES
MYSTERY MAGAZINE

VOLUME 3, NUMBER 2   Fall 2012

THE OUTBURSTS OF EVERETT TRUE

The Outbursts of Everett True was a two-panel newspaper comic strip created by A.D. Condo and J.W. Raper that ran from 1905 until 1927, when Condo was obliged to abandon it for health reasons. It's one of the comic strips that Sherlock Holmes could have read. We're running a few select panels in this issue.

PUBLISHER: JOHN BETANCOURT
EDITOR: MARVIN KAYE

Sherlock Holmes Mystery Magazine is published by Wildside Press, LLC. Single copies: $10.00 + postage. U.S. subscriptions: $39.95 (postage paid) for the next 4 issues in the U.S.A., from: Wildside Press LLC, Subscription Dept. 9710 Traville Gateway Dr., #234; Rockville MD 20850. International subscriptions: see our web site at www.wildsidemagazines.com. Available as an ebook through all major ebook etailers, or our web site, www.wildsidemagazines.com.

The characters of Sir Arthur Conan Doyle are used by kind permission of Jonathan Clowes, Ltd., on behalf of Andrea Punket, Administrator of the Conan Doyle Copyrights.

FROM WATSON'S SCRAPBOOK

For the past few months, Mr Sherlock Holmes has been having a right good chuckle at the expense of yours truly, but now that Mrs Hudson is at long last returned from her lengthy stay in Yorkshire, where she was assisting her Aunt Ruth to recover from a lingering illness, Holmes's risibility has finally been laid to rest. Be patient, dear friends, I will explain the circumstances directly.

In preparation for our preceding issue, *Sherlock Holmes Mystery Magazine #7*, Mrs H, though out of town, spoke on the telephone with Ms Carole Buggé about her writing under the pen-name of C. E. Lawrence. This interview, which began on page 18, was correctly titled: "C. E. Lawrence—The Darker Half of Carole Buggé"—conducted by [Mrs] Martha Hudson. But unfortunately some printer's devil saw fit to list said article on the Table of Contents page of *Sherlock Holmes Mystery Magazine #7* in this fashion: *Interview Conducted by* (Mrs) Martha Watson. (*N. B.: This has been corrected in subsequent copies.—MK*)

Martha *WATSON?!*

The error vastly amused Holmes, as I was made all too aware. A lesser mind might have laughed for a moment and let it go, but lately my friend has been in the doldrums, as it were, and with no investigations afoot, he devoted a surprising amount of time to devising all sorts of tomfoolery: advertisements from wedding-cake bakers; gift patterns registered for the "happy couple" at Gillow's; travel brochures pertinent to honeymooning in England, Ireland, Scotland, Wales (though not America). And so on … and on! Sophomoric, as I pointed out on more than one occasion, and yet, I admit, it was a most ingenious parade of practical jokery.

But now that Mrs Hudson is home again, the raillery has ceased, for Holmes has long respected our landlady's privacy. That she was married is evident in the pride with which she affixes that prefatory Mrs to her name, but further details of her domestic history are not open to discussion.

Out of curiosity I once asked her whether she had considered calling herself Ms Hudson, instead, but she replied, "No, Doctor, I do not particularly care for that term's sonority."

Speaking of Ms Buggé, I am pleased to announce that *The Star of India,* a splendid Holmesian adventure that she devised from my notes, and which was published some years ago by St Martin's Press, soon will be reissued in a British edition from Titan Publishing.

The current issue of *Sherlock Holmes Mystery Magazine* is chiefly devoted to American crime stories and their ilk; the only two Sherlock Holmes tales included are "The Man With the Twisted Lip," which I do believe is one of my friend's most amazing examples of his pure deductive genius, and "Sun Ching Foo's Last Trick."

—John H Watson, MD

✗　✗　✗　✗

I am planning to run an all-Holmes issue again in *Sherlock Holmes Mystery Magazine* #10 (as we did with SHMM #5). Thus, in our last editorial, we said we would include a delightful Holmes story by German writer Christian Endres in this issue, but we have decided to save it for SHMM #10. Instead we present "Sun Ching Foo's Last Trick," by Adam Beau McFarlane, which is shorter and fits better here.

So if you are not already a subscriber, now is an auspicious time to consider becoming one!

In regard to Carole Buggé, let me add to Dr. W.'s remarks that her C. E. Lawrence "Silent" series (an excerpt of which ran in SHMM #6) is still going strong. The latest title in this story of the investigations of a New York City forensic psychologist is about to appear: *Silent Slaughter;* its follow-up, *Silent Stalker,* is nearly finished . . . Carole a/k/a C. E. is an enormously prolific (and excellent) author.

✗　✗　✗　✗

Sherlock Holmes Mystery Magazine #8, I am happy to announce, features the latest installment in the exciting, often hilarious exploits of Harry Challenge, star of two novels and many shorter pieces by the estimable and also quite prolific Ron Goulart, as well as two new stories by our regulars, Marc Bilgrey and Bruce Kilstein. Dr. Kilstein has written some fine Sherlock Holmes pastiches, but this time he presents a fictionalized study of one of America's classically gruesome murders, the Lizzie Borden case. Another dark piece from newcomer Stefanie Stolinsky is based, the author says, on fact.

Finally, we are ever so glad to bring a new Kelly Locke case from Hal Charles in Kentucky, and the first of a new series of amusing detectival doings in John M. Floyd's "Traveling Light." Mr. Floyd's Lucy Valentine will be back with us again in *Sherlock Holmes Mystery Magazine* #9.

Canonically yours,
—Marvin Kaye

"Do you refuse to run pirated software?"

COMING NEXT TIME...

**STORIES! ARTICLES!
SHERLOCK HOLMES & DR. WATSON!**

Sherlock Holmes Mystery Magazine #9
**is just a few months away!
#10 will be another special Holmes Fiction Issue!**

Not a subscriber yet?
Send $39.95 for 4 issues (postage paid in the U.S.) to:
Wildside Press LLC
Attn: Subscription Dept.
9710 Traville Gateway Dr. #234
Rockville MD 20850

You can also subscribe online at
www.wildsidemagazines.com

SCREEN OF THE CRIME

by Lenny Picker

NOT A CARDBOARD BOX(ER), OR HOW MAKING MORIARTY A CHAMPION PUGILIST IN SHERLOCK HOLMES: GAME OF SHADOWS WON ME OVER TO THIS NONTRADITIONAL MOVIE SERIES

Caveat: As an anti-spoiler partisan who has written on the subject for *Publishers Weekly* ("Spoil the Plot, Or Spare the Riled," to promote myself shamelessly), I have decided to write this review in two parts—the first, without spoilers, the second, with some plot developments discussed in detail, for the many readers of *Sherlock Holmes Mystery Magazine* who will have seen the film by the time this column appears in print.

PART I

Color me astonished. I had reservations about Guy Ritchie's first Sherlock Holmes film, although I found aspects of it appealing. For all the efforts to find Canonical proof texts justifying that movie's depiction of Holmes more as an action hero than a quiet, patient thinker, both on the part of its production team and review-ers, it's clear that while that's an interesting reinterpretation of the Master, the emphasis should be on the "re." That's not just me; the DVD actually labels one of its special features, Sherlock Holmes Reinvented. Just as transforming Holmes into a Victorian Nero Wolfean (or Mycroftian) armchair reasoner distorts the character, making him a more intelligent precursor to James Bond, or a less affluent one than Bruce Wayne, also does so. I have generally been open to most variations on the character, from Christopher Plum-mer's appropriately-passionate and emotional portrayal in *Murder by Decree* in the face of corruption and horrific violence, to Nicol Williamson's paranoid cocaine addict in *The Seven-Percent-Solution*, and Benedict Cumberbatch's game-changing 21st century Sherlock. But 2009's Sherlock Holmes left me unsatisfied, and making Irene Adler into Holmes's Catwoman didn't quite do it for me.

So it was with considerable surprise—and pleasure—that I emerged from a screening of *Sherlock Holmes: Game of Shadows* very, very impressed. Parts of it were so well done that the movie has cracked my top-10 Holmes movie list (a ranking that does not include television adaptations such as the best of the Brett series, *The Patient's Eyes*, or *Sherlock*, and the subject of a future column). Let's be clear—this is not a return to the Holmes and Watson of the two Rathbone and Bruce films properly set in the Victorian era by any means. But this time, the extended fight scenes and campy exchanges between characters do not dominate. Instead, they take a back pew to one of the most, if not *the* most, compelling depic-tions, in any media, of the duel of the Titans that culminated in the Canon's "The Final Problem."

That is due to several elements, most notably an intelligent script that, plot- and pacing-wise, is much superior to the 2009 one, and Jared Harris's knockout characterization of the Napoleon of Crime. Faithful readers (if any, besides my long-suffering wife Chana) will recall that my last column discussed the challenges of presenting a Holmes-Moriarty battle of wits onscreen without changing the disgraced academic into more of a bloody hands-on master-criminal. Writers Michele and Kieran Mulroney, whose pre-vious credits are unfamiliar to me (*Paper Man*, or *Sunny and Share Love You*, anyone?) surmount all of them. (Especially-meaningless trivia: Kieran, who also acts, will be familiar to Seinfeld fans as "Timmy," whose line, to George Costanza, "You double-dipped the chip!" has entered popular culture.) The Mulroneys did so by not only incorporating dialogue straight from the Canon into Holmes and Moriarty's scenes together, but expand on the few glimpses of this influential and memorable villain in ways that not only suit the series's (and medium's) bias towards physical activity, but even eliminate a logical weakness in "The Final Problem" as Watson recounted it. More on that below.

No one before, to my knowledge, has truly tried to make the Professor an evil mirror-image of Holmes. This Moriarty is, like his archrival, a music buff devoted to opera. (One of the movie's emotional highpoints occurs during a performance in Paris of *Don Giovanni*.) His ability to anticipate and forestall Holmes's countermoves is impressively conveyed, and he remains several steps ahead of Holmes for much of the film. And, in an acceptable departure from Canon, the Mulroneys' Moriarty is still an active professor, a choice that makes his reputation as an upstanding citizen against whom Holmes has theories, but no proof, more comprehensible. Beyond that, we are shown the author of *The Dynamics of an Asteroid* lecturing, as well as autographing copies of his lecture notes.

Moreover, their Moriarty actually has an organization at his disposal, with Colonel Sebastian Moran as his able second-in-command. So, the Professor can sit back and plan for the most part, allowing others to do his dirty work, consistent with the role of the Canonical Moriarty.

Speaking of which, decades ago, I was troubled by the rationale behind the Moriarty of "The Final Problem's" choice to engage Holmes in physical combat at the Reichenbach Falls. He knew Holmes was an expert in baritsu, and his superior in the martial arts (and the other relevant "limits" he could have picked up on from a perusal of a certain 1887 Christmas Annual). Nor was Moriarty forced into a battle to the death because he had no one left to fight for him. Recall Holmes's words to a stunned Watson in "The Empty House" to explain the great hiatus—"I knew that Moriarty was not the only man who had sworn my death. There were at least three others whose desire for vengeance upon me would only be increased by the death of their leader. They were all most dangerous men." So, Moriarty knew that not only Moran had his back, but at least two others did as well. Why then, not have one of them give Holmes a fatal shove into the churning waters, if not pick him off from a safe distance with an airgun?

A much younger Lenny Picker speculated, as have others, that the Moriarty at Reichenbach was not *the* Moriarty, but a physically-superior impersonator. But the Mulroneys display their feel for the characters, and the spirit of the Canon, by making their Moriarty, who, like Downey's Holmes, is younger than usually presented (only Vincent D'Onofrio's criminal Napoleon in *A Case of Evil* was a younger man), the Cambridge boxing champion. By doing so, they continue the mirroring motif, and make it logical that the hyper-rational Moriarty would actually launch an assault on Holmes. (More on that in Part II, for those who've seen the movie). And they nicely set up the ending by having the famous first meeting between the arch-rivals occur in Moriarty's university office rather than at Baker Street.

The best-conceived and executed script in the world would be to no avail if the actor didn't fit the role. Fortunately, Jared Harris, son of the late Richard Harris (who played a Pinkerton agent infiltrating the Molly Maguires in the movie of that name), knocks it out of the park. Harris was a surprise choice for some, as better-known names were floated online, including Brad Pitt, Daniel Day-Lewis, Gary Oldman, and Javier Bardem. But it's hard to imagine anyone doing better. For me, Harris is right up there with Eric Porter, Michael Pennington, and George Zucco, conveying both menace and brilliance with subtlety and feeling.

Game of Shadows is more than Moriarty, of course. Jude Law continues to succeed as the "man of action" that Holmes dubs Watson in *The Hound of the Baskervilles*. His wedding to Mary Morstan is shown onscreen for perhaps the first time. Stephen Fry is as logical a Mycroft for our times as Robert Morley was in the 1960s. And, Downey's Holmes grew on me. Since this is a sequel, I was prepared for his manic portrayal that doesn't stint on Holmes's eccentricities.

The overall plot—Holmes trying to pull off the crowning achievement of his career by bringing the Professor to book—works. To those readers turned off by the first film, I say, give this one a chance, and perhaps, you, like me, will be pleasantly surprised, and eager to see how Sherlock Holmes 3 turns out.

PART II

Reminder—for those of you who passed lightly over my opening caveat—this section will reveal plot surprises that deserve to be experienced first by watching the movie.

As should be apparent by now, the movie works for me as a really good and intricate Holmes-Moriarty duel. The stakes are made plain early on, as Irene Adler, who worked for Moriarty in the first film, arranges to lunch with him in a very public place as a safety precaution after a botched assignment. But at a prearranged signal, all the other patrons empty the restaurant, leaving a poisoned Adler to collapse and expire without witnesses other than Moriarty and Moran.

Both Moriarty's disclosure of her fate to Holmes, and Watson's discovery of it, are masterfully handled—underplayed by the actors in a way that only makes the scenes stronger. That emotional undercurrent, absent in the first film, where Adler became, in part, a clichéd damsel-in-distress who needed rescuing from being sawed in half, is sustained, albeit with some interludes that are farcical rather than moving. The end, with the fatal tussle over the Reichenbach Falls was moving, an emotion not something I've generally associated with Holmes films, *Murder by Decree* notwithstanding.

And this Moriarty is no genteel criminal, as he's sometimes been portrayed, but a cruel sadist who doesn't mess around. In both *The Woman In Green* and *Hands of A Murderer*, Watson is lured away from 221B so the Professor can talk with Holmes without interruption, and returns unscathed once the conversation is over. This Moriarty, on learning that Holmes will not stand aside, torments Holmes by warning him that both the good Doctor and his new bride are fair game, despite Watson's intended retirement from crime-fighting. "The laws of celestial mechanics dictate that when two objects collide there is always damage of a collateral nature," the Professor observes, immediately before revealing that a rare form of tuberculosis has brought Irene Adler's life to an untimely end. And he doesn't hold back, sending a platoon of soldiers with tons of guns to shoot up the Watsons's railway carriage. His ultimate threat when his plans for a destabilizing political assassination at a peace summit are derailed, to find a creatively painful way to end the Watsons's lives, is again in keeping with an organized criminal leader responsible for immense human suffering, rather than a gentleman crook who plays by the rules.

Again, the lion's share of the credit for the film working as well as it did belongs to the writers. In an interview, the Mulroneys shared that apart from the producers giving them a bare plot concept—"taking the story outside London to the Continent and introducing the Moriarty character"—the story came from them. Even after others weighed in, the plotline "didn't really change from the first draft to the shooting script. What developed were the character relationships, the dialogue, of course, and the layering in of clues and details."

As to making Moriarty a boxing champion, the writers "knew from the outset that Moriarty must be Holmes's equal in intellectual terms, as he is in Doyle's books. Since our Holmes is a very physically capable character—a master of baritsu, also inspired by the books—we felt Moriarty should also possess great fighting prowess. Otherwise Holmes could too easily kick his behind! Both Guy Ritchie and Robert Downey are martial arts and boxing fanatics, so they led the charge to give Moriarty a boxing background. We very much wanted him to hide this skill set from Holmes until he absolutely needed to use it in their final confrontation. Holmes being Holmes, of course, he is one step ahead and knows of Moriarty's boxing past. So he is prepared mentally for what Moriarty throws at him."

Despite the mirror-imaging, the Mulroneys decided to differentiate Holmes and Moriarty in a more subtle way. "We wanted him to be a man of few words—as a counterpoint to Holmes's loquaciousness."

By succeeding in their goal of writing a "searingly intelligent, cold-blooded villain, who was both ruthless, unflappable, and for whom the game itself was almost as thrilling as the outcome," the Mulroneys provided material to match Harris's considerable gifts, and have set a standard that future Holmes-Moriarty duels, both on screen, and in print, must exert themselves to surpass.

Unfortunately from my point of view, but fortunately for them, the Mulroneys won't be back for the third Downey/Law film, as they are occupied with several other projects. They will be followed by British writer, Drew Pearce, who is also scripting Downey's third outing as Iron Man. With the Professor dead at the bottom of the Reichenbach Falls, creating a formidable adversary for Holmes next time will not be easy; while "the second most dangerous man in London," does survive Game of Shadows, the Mulroneys's version, much like the Canonical one, is more of a skilled hired gun, than an evil mastermind. And if Moriarty can be plausibly made into a man of action when needed, the same cannot be said for "the worst man in London," Charles Augustus Milverton. One of the other Moriarty brothers, perhaps? Or perhaps there was a second survivor of the fall into "that dreadful cauldron of swirling water and seething foam"? Whomever it is must be more like Harris's Moriarty than Mark Strong's Lord Blackwood of the first film.

Will the merits of Sherlock Holmes 2 continue in its sequel, or will it seem like just a fluke? We'll know in 2013.   ✗

Lenny Picker has been fascinated by Moriarty since reading "The Final Problem" at the age of thirteen, and staying up late to watch George Zucco in 1939's The Adventures of Sherlock Holmes. *He can be reached at chthompson@jtsa.edu.*

ASK MRS HUDSON

Dear Mrs. Hudson,

I am curious to know which is your favourite Sherlock Holmes story written by Dr Watson?

Peter

✗ ✗ ✗ ✗

Dear Peter,

What an intriguing question, and how difficult it is to answer! As I contemplate the question, half a dozen stories pop into my mind—"A Scandal in Bohemia," "The Adventure of the Dancing Man," "A Study in Scarlet" (I must confess a special fondness for the very first one, as a mother often has a special feeling for her first-born child.)

But then as I review this list, half a dozen more leap into my head, until my poor brain is quite muddled with the surfeit of choices. Very well, let me choose one and then tell you why I like it, if you will bear with me.

I shall choose "The Adventure of the Illustrious Client." In it, you may remember, Mr Holmes is engaged to keep the headstrong young Violet de Merville from making a disastrous marriage.

I think the tale demonstrates Holmes's reasoning ability as well as his fearlessness—he takes on the odious Baron Gruner, who promptly sends thugs to attack him. In spite of his expertise at single-stick combat, they do him considerable injury. There is a touching scene where dear Dr Watson visits the injured detective, fearing the worst, and Holmes soothes him, assuring the good doctor that the press has exaggerated his injuries.

The story also shows Mr Holmes's gallantry and tenderness toward women. It is true he does not trust them, but he has been misrepresented as loathing the sex entirely. Nothing could be further from the truth—no one is more solicitous or kinder to me than Mr Holmes, when the mood strikes him. Of course, he can be abrupt and dismissive, but that's as may be, and doesn't negate the many instances of his kindness. Otherwise, I should not have put up with his unorthodox behaviour for all these years, I can assure you!

I don't want to spoil the story for those of my readers who have yet to encounter it, but when the identity of the "illustrious client" was revealed, I must say I was quite thrilled, and my heart was quite aflutter for some time. I regard it as yet another tribute to my most unusual tenant—though Mr Holmes, bless him, took it quite in stride, as you may imagine.

Had he been half as impressed as Dr Watson and myself, I think he, too, would have taken pause to consider the honour it represented. But that's not Mr Holmes's way and never has been—he is of a most egalitarian disposition, and treats a stable groom with as much respect as a peer of the realm. A man ahead of his time in many ways, I always say, though I expect there are some who would take issue with me.

Although the doctor seldom speaks of it—I think for fear of embarrassing his friend—Mr Holmes is not without his admirers. I hope it's not telling tales out of school to relay an amusing incident involving a well-born young lady and her infatuation with Mr Holmes—that's the only word for it, I'm afraid—infatuation. She was quite besotted, and behaved with some forwardness, I'm afraid. Mr Holmes found himself in a rather delicate situation, which was compounded by Dr Watson's sincere desire to help his friend, though he did it rather clumsily, I'm afraid.

Of course I can't reveal the young lady's identity, but she was the sister of one of Mr Holmes's clients, and had occasion to meet him when he and Dr Watson paid a visit to their house. Lady W, as I shall call her, joined her brother for tea with the good doctor and Mr Holmes. She took a shine to Mr Holmes—apparently it was quite obvious, as Dr Watson himself remarked upon it. Mr Holmes alone dismissed it as "feminine charm" directed at everyone equally. That he did not perceive himself as the object of this young lady's affections further demonstrates his lack of understanding of matters of the heart.

Well, it seems that after the case was solved, Lady W contrived to "drop in" on my tenant, showing up at Baker Street in a very handsome carriage and four, if you can believe it! We don't see such extravagance in this part of London, I can tell you, and people were fairly hanging out of their windows to have a good look. The local street urchins fought with one another for the privilege of holding the horses while her Ladyship was inside, and although her coachman was quite capable of handling the situation, she gave them each half-a-crown! Bless me, but she was generous as well as extravagant.

Mr Holmes was out on a case, so I conversed with her briefly, until Dr Watson appeared, quite surprised to see her. I set out quite an impressive spread for tea, if I do say so myself, and we endeavoured to entertain her Ladyship as best we could. Mr Holmes was not due to arrive back at Baker Street for some time, and we certainly didn't expect her to take advantage of our hospitality and wait for him.

When it became clear that she was there to pursue a romantic interest in Mr Holmes—having no intention of engaging his professional services—Dr Watson embarked upon an ill-conceived attempt to dissuade her, engaging me as his unwilling accomplice.

"Ah, Mrs. Hudson," said he, "Holmes is still rather down in the dumps, don't you think?"

Not knowing what on earth he meant, I replied, "I suppose he is, if you think so."

The doctor then gave a mournful sigh, which sounded rather fake to me; I don't suppose he numbers acting among his many skills. I glanced at her Ladyship to see how she was receiving his rather amateur histrionics, but the keen expression on her face showed that she was very attentive, indeed. Dr Watson heaved another sigh, and I nearly burst out laughing, but he glared at me and I swallowed my mirth in a hastily-conceived coughing fit.

"It is indeed too bad," says he, "that the love of his life is in America, and not expected to return for some time yet."

My expression must have showed my utter astonishment at this pronouncement, but luckily the young lady was not looking at me. She leaned in toward the good doctor, so that her dainty hand nearly touched his.

"Is Mr Holmes married, then?"

"Married? No, I should think not," Dr Watson replied. "Though I daresay he wishes he were. The lady in question is not of a mind to marry—at least not at present, and not to him."

Lady W blushed most prettily and smiled, though even I could tell it was a forced smile. "I do not wish to pry," said she, though from her tone of voice and expression it was clear that was precisely her aim.

"Oh, it's no secret," the good doctor said with a wave of his hand. I daresay I was rather shocked to hear this claim, since it was not only a secret, it was a complete falsehood. "He is smitten with a lady of great birth and station in life, and she takes little notice of him. Still, he will entertain no other woman as a love interest, having given his heart to her. He is the kind of man who, once his troth is pledged, will remain forever faithful."

The young lady reddened. "If I had the good fortune to be loved by such a man as Mr Holmes, I should not treat him so lightly," she declared, her voice harsh with emotion.

"Your Ladyship is very kind," Dr Watson replied, pretending not to understand the sentiment behind her words. "I daresay you are a great deal more considerate than the young lady in question."

I offered more tea, which was refused, and our visitor soon took her leave of us, gliding down to her waiting carriage amidst the importuning of street waifs anxious to capitalize on her generosity. Dr Watson promised to give her regards to Mr Holmes, but I knew he would not tell of her visit unless he could not help it.

"Why, Dr Watson!" I exclaimed after the coach had driven off on the rain-slicked cobblestones. "I'm surprised at you! Lying to her Ladyship like that—whatever gave you the nerve to do such a thing?"

"My dear Mrs. Hudson," he replied, lighting a cheroot, "I wished to spare the young lady some embarrassment, and avoid putting Holmes in a delicate situation he is ill-equipped to handle. It seems to me a small lie is a small price to pay for such a thing."

Mr Holmes had the last word, though. When he arrived later that afternoon, with his usual alacrity and powers of observation, he deduced not only that we had had a visitor in his absence, but concluded correctly who it was. Dr Watson had no choice but to confirm his conclusions.

"And what did you tell her that caused her to depart so abruptly?" Holmes inquired.

Dr Watson nearly choked on his whisky. "How on earth did you know she—?"

Holmes gave a little laugh. "My dear fellow, when a woman hurries out of a room so quickly that she snags her expensive silk wrap on the door frame," he said, plucking a few cream-coloured threads from the door, "and furthermore, leaves her parasol," he added with a glance at the feather-trimmed accessory on the hearth, leaning against the mantel, "I can only conclude she left in some haste." He glanced at the table I was in the process of clearing. "Since she arrived in no particular haste—judging by the amount of tea and cakes she consumed—I can only conclude it was something you said that caused her to leave in such a flustered state of mind."

Dr Watson frowned and tossed his cigarette into the glowing embers of the fireplace. "Very well, Holmes, you win," he said, and proceeded to tell the entire story of Lady W's visit.

"Tut tut, Watson," Holmes said when he had finished. "I'm surprised you came up with a credible lie so readily. I do hope you aren't considering a future as a writer of agony columns."

"No chance of that," Watson muttered, moving to his writing desk.

"I am sorry you felt it necessary to lie to the young lady," Holmes remarked.

"I was merely trying to spare her—and you—considerable embarrassment," Watson said, clearly miffed. "I should think you'd be grateful."

"Hmm," said Holmes, turning to me. "Well then, Mrs Hudson, what have you for our dinner tonight? I'm quite famished."

"Lamb chops," I replied. "Either that or Welsh rarebit. Take your pick."

"I'm not hungry," Watson declared moodily.

"Come along, my dear fellow, dine with me, won't you?" said Holmes. Things had evidently gone well for him today, for he was in a jovial mood.

"I shouldn't think you'd want to have dinner with a liar," Watson grumbled.

"Goodness, Watson," Holmes said. "If there's one thing I've learned about human nature, it's that everybody lies. You told a lie today that you hoped would help me out, and for that I should be grateful. Never mind whether it was the right thing to do or not—you did your best as you saw it."

"Very well," Watson said. "Next time I'll let you fend for yourself when a woman like that practically throws herself at you."

"If you must," Holmes said. "But for God's sake, next time you give me a fictional lady friend, would you do me a favour and put her somewhere else other than America? I mean, if you want your story to be credible. Who on earth would leave England to go there?"

"Yes, I supposed you're right," said Watson. "Mrs Hudson, I think I'll have the Welsh rarebit, if you don't mind."

"And I'll have the chops," Holmes proclaimed. "If that's not too much trouble for you."

"No," said I. "It's no trouble at all."

✗ ✗ ✗ ✗

Thank you again for your letter, Peter—please write again sometime.

Very truly yours,
Mrs Hudson

✗

SCENES FROM LITTLE KNOWN SHERLOCK HOLMES STORIES

∘ APOTHECARY ∘

MARC BILGREY

"ID LIKE TO BUY A SEVEN PERCENT SOLUTION OF COCAINE... ON SECOND THOUGHT IM TRYING TO CUT DOWN, SO GIVE ME A PACK OF GUM, INSTEAD."

SHERLOCK HOLMES AND THE CASE OF THE GERMAN SERIALS

by Gary Lovisi

The strange case I am about to relate to you, gentle reader, began in the last days of a cold December morning in the year of '09—that is—in the year 2009! That was when my wife, Lucille, presented me with a rather odd and certainly unique Sherlockian book as a Christmas gift. She knows I am enamored of nearly everything pertaining to Holmes, no matter how odd or scarce, and this book certainly fit the bill. However, what I did not know at the time was that this book would lead to my discovery of an entire realm of hitherto unknown Holmes books to me—which I now seek to share with you.

The large hardcover book was simply titled "Sherlock Holmes" embossed in gold leaf with the mysterious initials "V.B." in the lower right corner, the only other information on the otherwise dark green simulated leather hardcover binding. There was no jacket. However, as intriguing as the title and mysterious initials were upon the cover of this ancient tome (I guess I should mention now that the book is from 1907 and well over 100 years old!), what was inside I found much more fascinating.

The book conained 12 individual Sherlock Holmes German dime novel type serials from 1907, bound together. I had never seen their like before but I was instantly fascinated by them, excited to find out more. It was not easy. The text was written in German, and I do not speak or understand the German language. However, some information was discernible from simple Holmesian observation, so I put the Master's techniques to use to garner what facts I could.

This is a series of German dime novel type booklets entitled *Detektiv Sherlock Holmes und Seine Weltbreuhmten Abventeur*—which roughly translates into English as "Sherlock Holmes Most Famous Cases"—though another translation has it as "Detective Sherlock Holmes and His World-Famous Adventures." Issue #1 is dated January 2, 1907 and is entitled *Das Geheimnis Jurgen Witwe*—or "The Mystery of the Young Widow." Each 32-page issue sold for 20 pfenning, measured roughly 8.5 x 10.5 inches, or quarto size, and were published weekly in Germany. The covers featured really wonderful full color illustrations, many depicting Holmes and his 'companion' (more on this soon). There is also a small cover box with an illustration of the profile of the Great Detective smoking his ever-present pipe looking on in serious deductive thought.

The color cover art for these booklets is just terrific. Issue #1 shows an unmistakable Holmes in the sitting room at 221B standing before a soldier and his wife giving his deduction to their problem with his usual aplomb. A traditional image of what appears to be Dr. Watson is seated behind him at a desk. Issue #4 shows Holmes with a revolver, shocked as he grabs at a criminal's arm—only to

discover it detached from the man's body, it is a prosthetic. That issue is a reprint, you may note the new title for the series. Issue #8 shows a startled and weeping woman, whom having removed a painting from where it was hanging upon the wall, reveals a hidden skeleton! It is most effective, as are many of the other covers in this series.

As I did more research on this lovely and fascinating book I began to discern more interesting facts about the series and the stories themselves. The most interesting being that the 12 stories I had in my book (all written in German, in a heavy Gothic font reminiscent of pre-World War I type), were not only all Sherlock Holmes stories—but *none* of them seemed to be Doyle stories! Even though my knowledge of the German language is severely limited I was able to discover this by going through the text of each story line-by-line looking for familiar names from The Canon. I found none. These are, in fact, all new Holmes tales. What I had found were original stories featuring an entirely new set of characters who had come to Holmes with new cases for him to solve—none of which were created by Doyle.

Even more startling to me was the discovery that while Holmes was indeed present in every story in dialog and in quotations, I could not find hide nor hair of his trusty companion, Dr. John H. Watson. Watson, it seemed did not exist in these stories at all! I was astounded. Then who was telling the stories? Well, I soon discovered that the narrator to these 12 tales was an apparently new companion and chronicler of the Great Detective—and that was the young and dashing Harry Taron—in some incarnations called "Taxson," though the name is difficult for me to make out in the old Gothic German script. Taron is noted in the text as *der famulus von Sherlock Holmes*—or "the friend of Sherlock Holmes." So, bye-bye Watson! Hello Harry! There is even a drawing of Harry on the first page of the third issue from January 30, 1907, for the story titled *Das Ratfel am Spieltifche*. He looks nothing like Watson at all.

There are in fact, two series, where a new one continues after the first. After issue #10, the series suddenly takes on a new title and drops the name "Sherlock Holmes". I wondered why? Well, it seems that by issue #10 there was some concern (some researchers even call it wrath) by the lawyers for Sir Arthur Conan Doyle that

the name of Sherlock Holmes was used in this series, so it was taken out of the title from issue #11 on.

The new title of the series became *Ausdem Geheimakter des Weltdetektius* or "The Secret Files of The King of Detectives." Nevertheless, while the name of the Great Detective was deleted from the title of the series, nor was the name of Holmes used in the titles of any of the individual stories, he is unabashedly present under his true name in *every* story—along with his faithful companion and chronicler—Harry Taron!

The series was published by Verlagshaus fur Volksliteratur und Kunst (The Publishing House for Popular Fiction and Art), in Berlin. They had been successful with publishing *groschenromane*, the

German equivalent of the dime novel (or penny dreadful). I was further interested to discover that those first issues were noted in English as being published under "privilege of copyright in the United States of America reserved under the Act approved March 3, 1905." I believe that this means the German publisher contracted with and bought the rights to the character from the American reprinter of Sherlock Holmes, *not* from Doyle and his British publisher. I think that is the reason for the problem with Doyle's lawyers (Doyle was after all alive at this time and still writing his own new Holmes tales), so his lawyers insisted the title of this German series be changed. It was. Though of course the German publisher never eliminated Sherlock Holmes from any of the stories. A rather neat trick of copyright infringement. In fact, during this era, Doyle's Sherlock Holmes appeared in quite a few so-called "pirates," or pirated book editions in America and other countries where Doyle received no payment. I can only imagine Sir Arthur's frustration, and the fact that his solicitor must have had a full-time job insisting upon the protection of Doyle's literary rights, as well as payment for the use of his creation or for reprinting stories in those long ago days before international copyrights, and almost a century before Holmes would legitimately enter the public domain.

As I continued my investigation into this amazing area of Germanic Holmesia, I made use of various helpful sources on the Internet that really opened my eyes to what had gone on here regarding this early unauthorized version of Sherlock Holmes in Europe. This is being done, you must remember, all while Doyle was still alive and it must have been a constant source of irritation to him.

What I discovered next shocked and surprised even myself. For I soon learned that my copies of the first 12 issues of the rare booklets in my hardcover book were only the tip of the iceberg of this strange story. For with booklets apparently being published each week from January, 1907 until June, 1911—I discovered there were an amazing *230* issues in this series! Truly an incredible accomplishment. Each 32-page issue features a *new* Sherlock Holmes and Harry Taron mystery adventure with a wonderful color cover drawing depicting a key scene from the story. For instance, issue #36 shows a dockyard scene as one

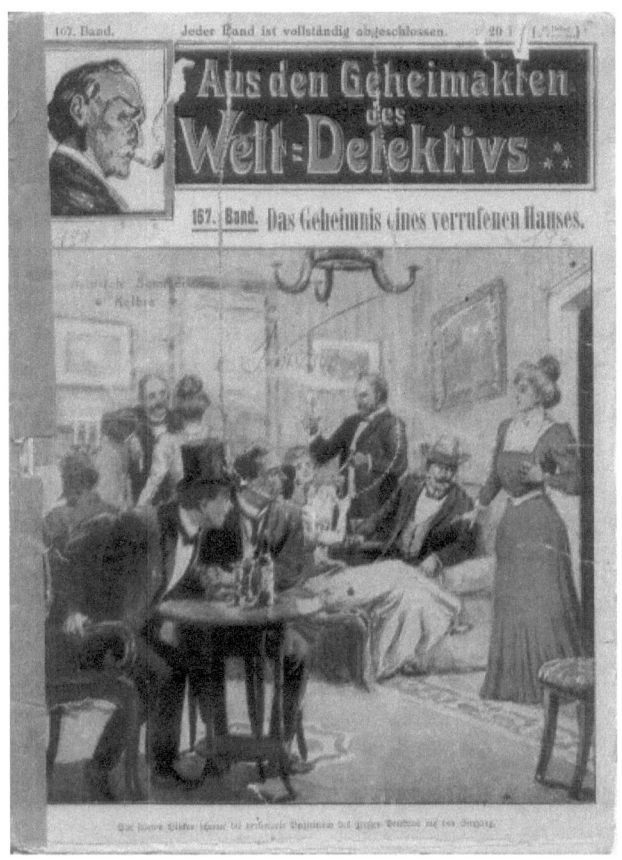

man attacks another with a revolver—perhaps Holmes arresting a villain? While on issue #41 we see Holmes versus a ghastly ghostly image. There are many more covers and all the art is interesting and exciting. Even if you can not read the German stories, these books can be enjoyed for the cover art alone. The main character in all issues of the series is undoubtedly Sherlock Holmes, who is still the solver of amazing crimes and investigates problems that the police can not crack.

It's an intriguing series for any Holmes fan or the lover of pastiche, and while these stories have lately been reprinted by Doyle's German publisher into a series of 34 best-selling paperbacks, I do not believe they have ever appeared in English. That is a shame. I would really love to have the opportunity to read one of these tales in English to see how these early German writers treated the Great Detective and his cases. However, with a new Holmes story appearing in Germany every week in this series, the German publisher had to have a stable of reliable professional writers always at hand—who also had to write *fast*—able to meet incredibly tight deadlines quickly. Certainly none of them could have been as good as Doyle? Or could they? My assumption is that with 230 stories written by various writers, they must be of varying quality. However, this series was extremely popular and lasted five years, so the stories must have had positive aspects going for them other than merely containing the character Sherlock Holmes. Whether this is the case or not, it kind of makes me wonder what it might be like to read one of them today in English—in a decent translation, of course.

The strange tale of these German Sherlock Holmes stories does not stop here. In October of 1907, 16 of the original German stories were adapted into French by the publisher Fernand Laven. Later on, in 1927, a Dutch publisher did their version of the German stories, this time under the title *Harry Dickson de Amerikaansche Sherlock Holmes* or "Harry Dickson, the American Sherlock Holmes." Holmes was now changed to Dickson and now became American! Holmes remained Dickson from then on. In this new version Holmes (or I should say, Dickson) still has his assistant, but now the assistant's name has been changed yet again, now from Harry Taron to Tom Wills. This Dutch series lasted 180 issues until May, 1935.

Also in 1928, Belgian publisher Janssens had author Jean Ray translate the Dutch series into French and the well-known French-language editions of *Harry Dickson, le Sherlock Holmes Americain*, began in January, 1929 and ran 178 issues until April, 1938, just before World War II began and Paris fell. Ray soon began writing original stories published with cover art supplied by noted German artist Alfred Roloff. Roloff's excellent artwork is said to have inspired Ray's desire to write new stories. In France, Harry Dickson's fame is said to rival that of Arsene Lupin and even the great Sherlock Holmes himself.

While these various series may be fodder for another day, it is worthy to note that the beginnings of Sherlock Holmes pastiche in Europe began over a hundred years ago in Germany, way back in 1907 with a lovely little series of dime novel booklets—or as I have put it—with Sherlock Holmes and the case of the German serials.

✗

SUN CHING FOO'S LAST TRICK

by Adam Beau McFarlane

An unseasonably hot June brought a feverish outbreak of criminal activity, leaving Scotland Yard busy and Holmes cataloguing newspaper articles into albums with paste and scissors. Countless visitors had presented their problems at 221 Baker Street. But that summer, without any client asking him to, Holmes solved a man's killing after we witnessed it with our very own eyes.

The sun lasted late on Whitmonday and Mary was visiting family, so I asked Holmes to join me at a variety show featuring Sun Ching Foo, the conjurer. I'd hoped that a magic show of impossible acts would entertain a man whose trade was explaining mysteries. With his straw hat and walking stick, he joined me for an evening's entertainment.

The hall's benches were crowded with people from all walks of life. The stage was ornately decorated and rigged with curtains. We sat through singers, dancers, and jugglers, and we ate our way through a series of roasted peanuts, Chelsea buns, and peppermint water. Sun Ching Foo was saved for the big finish—though little did we know how big it would be.

Wearing an electric blue robe embroidered with golden stars and moons, Sun levitated his assistant and plucked white hares from his wizard's cap. His assistant, Lai Way, wore a black gown and long sable hair. Her Oriental face was yellow with dark eyes.

The grand finale was the famous bullet-catching trick. Lai Way asked for a volunteer who was a soldier or a former soldier. I raised my hand. She stepped down and waded into the crowd, picking a man and asking him to go to the stage.

While the soldier made his way forward, she asked for another volunteer. She was not near me, but I raised my hand again. Sherlock looked at me with a slight smile of amusement.

Again, I was not picked. The new volunteer marked a bullet. Lai Way thanked him, dropped the bullet into a pail, then walked the pail to the stage.

When Lai Way reached the volunteering soldier who was now onstage, he introduced himself as Alastair Franklin.

She picked the bullet from the pail. "Is this reel bullet, Alastair?" she asked in halting English. He agreed. Then Way asked, "You see how it marked with skrachis?" He agreed again.

Excitement bubbled inside me. I'd seen the trick before: the volunteer would load a gun and shoot it at Sun Ching Foo. But Sun would catch the bullet in his hand and show it to the soldier, who would recognize it by the scratches made by the other volunteer in the crowd. I thought, let Holmes try and explain this!

Alastair Franklin and Lai Way stood at the left end of the stage. Sun stood on the right end. The assistant handed Franklin a rifle. It resembled the jezail that ended my career in the Army, except this one was white, inlaid with bone or ivory and studded with jewels.

She produced black powder and a ramrod. Angling the gun upright on the stage,

Franklin poured black powder down the muzzle into the barrel. He pushed in the bullet.

Way handed him the ramrod, then he moved the bullet and powder down the barrel.

Once the ramrod was shoved from end to end of the barrel, she motioned for the ramrod. Franklin gave it back, and she stepped away, fading into the shadows in the back of the stage.

He cocked the gun and loaded a percussion cap under the hammer. As Franklin raised the gun, the band begun to play. A drum roll reeled through the air. "Ready!" Sun Ching Foo called out. "Aim!" The soldier settled the gun against his shoulder and peered down the length of the barrel. The wizard shouted, "Fire!"

The shot exploded off the walls as Sun Ching Foo dropped to his knees and cried out, "Thomasina!"

I looked at Holmes, who had a look of uncertainty on his face, then I grabbed his arm and the curtain began to descend.

"Watson, what are you doing?"

"That was not supposed to happen—he really was shot."

When we reached the stage, Sun lay face-up on the boards with blood coating his costume. "I'm a doctor!" I exclaimed. Tearing the silk, I pulled brass buttons apart from their loops. The bullet had passed through him, leaving a wound hole in his abdomen through to his back.

The stage curtain was a scrim. On the far side of it, we could see the orchestra, the rows of chairs, and the exit doors in the back. The musicians struck up "God Save the Queen" and then the audience stood up to sing.

Sun gasped for air, choking. He coughed and splashed blood from his mouth, then he was dead. His head dropped against the floor, knocking his hat off. His queue severed from his head as a black cloth band slipped from its concealment under against his hairline. Looking at his face, I saw that his complexion and Oriental features were a careful artifice of cosmetics.

I closed his eyelids and looked up. Peering over me, Inspector Lanners stood beside Holmes. "I was in the audience," he said.

The stage was a grim scene as we huddled around the corpse. People filed out of the theatre. While the body of Sun Ching Foo lay still, couples were holding hands and mothers towed away their entertained children.

Holmes searched the stage. He took out his pocket lens and hovered around the wall. "Lanners," he said, "the bullet has lodged itself," he said, pointing. Holmes pried it from the lincrusta wallpaper and turned it around under the magnifying glass. The weapon that pierced Sun Ching Foo had been rendered into a shapeless lump of metal.

"Could it have been from another gun? Someone in the audience or secreted near the stage?" Lanners asked.

Holmes shook his head. "We would have heard a separate shot fired. Sun Ching Foo must have been killed by his own gun; otherwise, the report from another fire-arm would have revealed itself. No marksman could have timed his gun to have fired simultaneously."

"Would you be willing to join us at Scotland Yard?" Lanners asked.

"I wouldn't have it any other way," Holmes responded.

⤬ ⤬ ⤬ ⤬

The constabulary took the soldier and Sun Ching Foo's stagehand to Scotland Yard while we followed in a cab. The new Metropolitan Police building was two levels of grey granite lifting red and white stripes of bricks. Windows in gables and dormers looked out from an additional five floors. Lamps along the Victoria Embankment glowed in the settling dusk.

After we arrived, Lanners allowed us to meet with Alastair Franklin. The large man had side whiskers linked to his moustache. White hairs sprouted from his blond hair and his skin had a tanned complexion.

Holmes asked, "Did you know Sun Ching Foo? Any business or relationship with him?"

"No, inspector."

Holmes held up his hand. "Just Mister Holmes. Had you seen him before?"

"I'm in the navy, just returned from Alexandria the day before last. My wife and our son were at the show—they'll be wondering what happened to me, I expect." Despite his sturdy build, his hands trembled anxiously. "I don't know what happened upon the stage; all I did was as I was told."

"Did you know that you would be selected from the crowd?"

He shrugged his shoulders, lifting his palms up, while shaking his head. "Now how would I know that?"

Holmes turned to Lanners and asked, "Where is the gun?"

After locking the sailor into an interrogation room, the inspector led us to an office where the muzzleloader laid across a desk. The rifle butt was pentagonal with an upward curve. The whole stock was painted white and fastened with shiny buttons that looked like jewels.

"These extra screws hold an exceptionally pronounced ramrod holder substituted for the original one." Holmes pointed to a slender tube beneath the barrel, running from breech to muzzle.

Lanners opened the door and ushered in the conjurer's assistant. She remained wearing a black cossack. Lai Way sat then she removed her wig. Her red-gold titus hair contrasted with the cascade of her brunette wig.

"You are not Chinese, either?" I said.

Lai Way agreed. "We have been Hindoos, Muhammedans, and Injuns. Sun Ching Foo was my husband. His real name is Cecil Windham."

"You must be Thomasina, the name he called out," Holmes said.

She nodded as she rubbed her face. The make-up that darkened her complexion and drew out her eyes smeared away.

"How did you meet him?" Holmes said.

"I was a showgirl in America and Cecil hired me as assistant. When he came to London, he became Sun Ching Foo."

"How does the bullet-catching trick work?" Holmes asked.

"I don't know. Cecil never explained the trick to me," she said.

"What was supposed to happen?" he said.

"He was supposed to catch the bullet in his hand."

"But you cannot catch a bullet in your hand!" Lanners exclaimed.

The assistant shrugged. "Cecil did."

"Tell me about your part in the trick," Holmes said.

"A man in the crowd marks the bullet. As I walk to the stage, I switch the bullet with a different one. The one that I replace it with has my own markings. Then, when the bullet is fired, Sun Ching Foo catches the bullet. He shows it to the soldier—and it's the same one that I have marked."

"Is this the bullet?" Holmes reached into his pocket and held out his fist. Unfurling his fingers, he revealed a minie ball.

Thomasina's face went white. "How … how did you … ?"

"It was clutched in his hand while Watson attempted to save him. Clearly, the bullet was not meant to kill but instead, he was to hold up his bullet as if the shot traveled from the barrel and into his grasp."

"Then where was the bullet from the gun supposed to go?" she asked.

"Perhaps the soldier was to fire away and not actually strike Sun Ching Foo?" Lanners asked.

"You mean, somehow the soldier's aim would be off?" Holmes said.

Lanners mused. "Could Sun Ching Foo have created some kind of illusion, so the soldier would not be actually aiming properly?"

"That's no better than saying 'magic'," Holmes said.

Thomasina agreed. "I have been part of every performance of the trick, but I noticed no changes to the stage."

"Perhaps it was supposed to be arranged? Perhaps the soldier was a confederate?" I said.

"We already talked to the solider. I am convinced of his innocence." Holmes said.

I added, "Perhaps there was a confederate in the audience. Someone who would have fired away from Sun Ching Foo. But rather, she picked someone else."

"No, sir! This is not true," Thomasina said.

"Perhaps someone uncovered his American identity?" I asked.

Holmes shook his head. "And this person knew the secret to the magic trick and, moreover, had enough access to bedevil it? I think it unlikely." He continued speaking. "Did Windham have any enemies?"

She shook her head. "His only concern was other conjurers who had more business than he."

"What about enemies within the show? You or his other assistants?"

"Not at all, Mister Holmes. I was a poor showgirl with nothing in America. When Cecil met me, he could barely afford to pay me and buy food for himself ... but together, we made something special, didn't we?" A tear caught the light sparkling in her eye.

Lanners spoke up. "Go home and rest, everyone. We'll learn no more tonight. Come back tomorrow and we can continue with refreshed eyes."

"A man was killed in front of us. Can I rest, Watson?" Holmes crushed his straw hat between two fists.

We returned to Baker Street very late. I agreed to stay the night, just like old times. As soon as we finished breakfast the next morning, the pageboy presented Thomasina Windham. She removed her bonnet with trembling hands.

"Please Mister Holmes, you must help me. I am at your mercy," she said.

Sherlock walked over from the fireplace and greeted her. "Calm your nerves and we can discuss the matter."

Before taking a seat, Thomasina stepped over to the window, eyeing the back garden and the long shadows cast by the low morning sun.

We reclined into chairs while our guest's nerves settled with a glass of brandy. She told Holmes, "I wish to hire your services."

I took the brandy bottle off the mantel, re-filled her glass, then returned it to its position beside a bowl of lilies and a vase of peacock feathers.

Holmes said, "How can we help you, madam?"

"The police suspect me."

"I do not think so."

"But they will, Mister Holmes, they will! It's on account that I wish to sell the Sun Ching Foo show to Miles Cavendish, a rival magician. For years, Mister Cavendish has tried to buy Cecil's tricks or to pay for a stake. Now, I want to offer him everything—the props, the staff, the future bookings."

"And they will see this as profiting from Cecil's death? A profit that led you to kill him in the first place?" Holmes said. "How much money do you stand to make?"

Tears broke her face. As she wiped away face powder, I saw wrinkles worried into her face with age. Her lashes matted together in anguish. She wanted to speak, but her breath caught in short gasps.

"The show is worth nothing to me. Cecil was heavily indebted. Sale of everything will be enough to pay off his debts, but little more. The Sun Ching Foo act has been a success, but Cecil financially ruined us. He piled together bills and spent on credit in the company of women that I do not care to speak of. I am ruined! Just look at the newspapers!"

She slapped down *The Morning Mirror*. Its broadside read "CONJURER'S WIFE KILLS HIM DURING FINAL PERFORMANCE."

"They'll use someone else's name tomorrow," I assured her. "Better yet, this paper will forget the story and *The Evening Mirror* will accuse someone else."

"Do you think he planned this? Did he take his own life?" Holmes asked.

"I wish I knew, although I don't think so. He is not the kind of person to contemplate such a death. He does not give into bursts of emotion. Not even when angry or upset."

"Perhaps he was the opposite, and was quiet or withdrawn as of late?"

"He is in fine spirits lately. He is as talkative and even-keeled as ever. Oh, Mary help me, I can't bring myself to say 'he *was*' anything. 'He *is*' to me—he can't be gone. I cannot allow it." She began to cry again. "But we are in such debt! If I do not accept that he is gone, the collectors will take the last crumb from my pantry."

Holmes sighed. "Send Miles Cavendish inside."

Her crying sputtered to a stop. "How do you know?"

"You looked outside, I assume a man is waiting. If it isn't Miles Cavendish, then surely you are followed."

She went to the window and opened it, then she gestured. Minutes later we were joined by a stranger. He had a tiny beard growing at the tip of his chin in the fashion of Disraeli, but it started directly under his lip and sprouted downward. His eyes were black and deep-set.

"Ah, the Amazing Cavendish!" Holmes remarked. "With the signature 'Vanishing Lady' act. A fellow conjurer, perhaps it was you who killed Sun Ching Foo?"

His face frowned. "I assure you, nothing can be further from the truth. Sun Ching Foo was no friend, but he was no enemy, either. Suggesting I killed Sun Ching Foo for his business is like me suggesting that you should kill Lestrade to snatch more cases to solve."

Holmes chuckled. "Very well, who do you think killed him?"

"A spurned lover, angry creditors, or even himself? If he committed suicide, shouldn't we search for a note?"

"If he committed suicide, then what is the mechanism? Thomasina, you say you don't know how the trick worked, but how did he set it up?" Holmes asked.

She shrugged her shoulders. "I don't know. We all had tasks to do—I was preparing other things while he was working on the gun."

Holmes asked, "Did he do anything to the guns after a performance?"

She nodded. "Why yes! See, the gun was not meant to fire. So every night, Cecil took apart the rifle to extract the bullet. He would shake the powder out and put that back in the container, too."

"Usually, the gun did not fire? If it wasn't supposed to, then how did Cecil simulate the sound of shooting?"

She shrugged. "It was all part of the magic of Sun Ching Foo."

"Where was he before the show? What was he doing?"

Thomasina was quiet; instead, Cavendish spoke up. "Sun Ching Foo was in the company of a woman besides his wife."

"How is it that you know this?" Holmes asked.

"His colourful social habits were known to all at the Bixby Club, of which we were both members."

"It is imperative that I question this woman, Mister Cavendish. Give her name to the Yard, and they will bring her in for questioning."

Holmes turned to Thomasina. "You ask for help, madam, and I shall offer it. But even without your plea, I would see this through to the end. A man has died in front of my eyes. The honor of my trade is at stake."

Jealousy, anger, vengeance – I saw none of that on the wife's face. She showed only silent despair. "Thank you, Mister Holmes."

We returned to the Metropolitan Police. Parliament's clock tower looked at us over St. Stephen's House. Lanners explained to Holmes that the woman was found, and they discussed what questions had been posed already and her answers. Once Holmes had his fill of the information, Lanners walked us to the same room where Alastair Reynolds had been questioned.

Inside the office, she waited. I will spare this woman her decency by concealing a name, but I shall describe her as a young Scotch-woman wearing a Norfolk jacket with leg-of-mutton sleeves and a skirt. Her hair curled loosely over greenish-blue eyes.

"Questions from one constable were not enough, now he brings two more?" she muttered.

"I am Sherlock Holmes, an independent consulting detective, and this is Doctor John Watson, who attended Cecil Windham in the final moments of his life."

"Well? What do you want with me?"

"How long did you know Sun Ching Foo?"

"Since the start of the summer," she said. "When he first began performing his show, he found me working in a laundry and invited me to see a matinee for free. When I went, I didn't know he was Sun Ching Foo. But calling on me afterward, he told me—and amused me with his sleight-of-hand."

"Think carefully now, miss. Did he promise you anything?" His stare grew intense.

She rolled her eyes and laughed. "All men promise, Mister Holmes. Cecil was no different."

"But what did he promise you?"

"That he loved me, that we could be together. He wanted to set up a touring company and travel with me. First, to Scotland, and then to the Continent or to South America. He promised that we could be happy together."

"And what about his wife?"

She looked away. "I knew he was married, but he never mentioned her. And I never asked. I said that all men promise, but I don't think that they keep their promises."

"Did you know that his wife lived with him, here in London?"

She shrugged noncommittally.

"A Chinese woman who could not speak the language, who knew nothing of our land or culture?"

She grimaced and her gaze fell. "Please stop, you make me ill. I am ashamed."

He muttered quietly, "The poor woman has no family here nor a penny in her own name. She will most likely die in the gutter. She is a prisoner without walls." Then Holmes's voice grew hard as steel. "Your womanly scheme killed her husband, the one man she trusted with her wretched life!"

A whimpering cry erupted from the woman's lips. "No, Mister Holmes! I will confess all of my sins to you, but I didn't hold plans against Cecil! I had nothing to do with it! I beg you to believe me!" She threw her hands over her face and cried.

Holmes looked at Lanners. "Take her away. She is of no use to us."

As he escorted her out of the office, I remarked, "Holmes, you are a cold-blooded liar."

"Nevertheless, I produced the truth in her. We should re-examine the gun next."

Lanners returned and led us back to the jezail. Holmes held it up and inspected it, turning it around in his hands.

"These screws seem strangely placed," he said. He reached into his satchel for tools, then slowly removed the screws. Without them, the barrel and ramrod tube fell away from the breech.

He picked up a screw and carefully eyed the threads, then he focused his magnifying glass upon the holes in the pieces of rifle.

"Eureka, gentlemen!" Holmes chuckled and reassembled the jezail.

A mixture of puzzlement and relief washed over Lanners's face. "What is it Holmes?"

"The soldier, Alastair Dayton, loaded gunpowder and the bullet," Holmes said, sliding a finger from the hole down the length of the barrel.

"Yes, go on," Lanners said.

"The rifle's firing mechanism, however, is blocked off from the barrel. Instead, it looks connected to this tube which, as I remarked yesterday, is bigger than a ramrod holder." He touched the extra compartment.

I nodded. "And Lai Way – Thomasina – took the ramrod back. The soldier didn't rest it there after the bullet was loaded. The gun itself was part of the trick?"

"Right. This was an extra firing chamber. There must have been gunpowder inserted here by Sun Ching Foo before the show. When the trick works correctly, a soldier pulls the trigger and the powder in this chamber ignites. But the powder in the barrel remains untouched."

"So what happened in this case?" Lanners asked.

"It starts with the use of an old gun. The false chamber and real barrel must have been assembled years ago. To hold them together against the breech of the stock, holes were drilled in. The screws go from the stock, through the extra chamber, and into the barrel. Slowly, rust accumulated between the screw and the holes holding the pieces together."

Lanners's gaze became unfocused. "All very interesting, Holmes but—"

"Patience, inspector! As I was saying, when that connection deteriorated, a slight opening formed. Gunpowder from the barrel leaked into the hole where the screws fastened the gun together. Sun Ching Foo never cleaned it properly, but he just shook out the powder. Over time with successive performances, excess particles accumulated to form a charge through the hole. So now, when the flash from the percussion cap travelled down to the secret chamber, it also went up into the barrel. Thus, the whole gun shot off and the bullet was fired."

To prove his point, Holmes took a pitcher of water off the desk and slowly poured water down the barrel. After a moment, drops dripped from the attached tube. "Poor Cecil Windham had no idea what happened when he died."

By day's end, Lanners released Alastair Dayton. Cecil Windham's body returned to the United States with his widow later that month.

By the next morning, newspapers barely mentioned Sun Ching Foo. There was no mention of his wife, nor any mention of Holmes, either.

He laughed. "An error I'm sure you will correct!" Closing his eyes with a smile, he said, "I've helped countless people, Watson, but I don't expect to be remembered. No, the only memories made on Baker Street will be from Madame Tussaud's waxen people or in a childhood visit to the zoo in Regent's Park."

I chuckled with him, promising to myself to write this adventure some day to ensure the memory of Sherlock Holmes as well as the tragic death of the man London knew as Sun Ching Foo.

✗

DO YOU LOVE ME?

by Marc Bilgrey

"Do you love me?" asked Jan.

"Of course, I love you," replied Bob, pulling the sheet over their naked bodies and fluffing up his pillow.

"Then why won't you leave your wife?" she asked.

Bob sighed and looked over at the painting of a Paris street that hung near the bed. It was one of those garish pictures you only see in cheap motel rooms. Which made perfect sense, since that's exactly where he was.

"Do we have to have this discussion every time we meet?" asked Bob.

"Well, when else can we have it? It's not like I can call you at your apartment or meet you at work."

"There's nothing to talk about. If I leave her, I'm left with no money."

"I've finally figured out a solution."

"A solution?" Bob reached over to the night table and picked up a container of bottled water that he'd bought from the soda machine down the hall, and took a sip.

"Yes, you kill her."

"Oh, that's a great idea," said Bob, rolling his eyes.

"I'm serious."

"Are we going to spend the next couple of hours making love or waste our time talking over ridiculous ideas?"

"There's nothing ridiculous about it. Will you hear me out?"

"I guess I don't have much of a choice."

"How about you lose the attitude for five minutes."

Bob sighed. He hated when she got like this. Why couldn't she just accept things the way they were? Why did she constantly pester him on the subject? Things were fine. He saw Jan a couple of times a week, usually after work. Why push it? But, he decided, if Jan wanted to talk, there was nothing he could do about it.

"You kill your wife and blame it on a burglary gone bad," said Jan.

"Oh?" replied Bob, stifling a yawn.

"You walk in and find her dead."

"And how does she die?"

"It's very simple." Jan reached into her purse and pulled out a gun.

"Where'd you get that?"

"Never mind, just take it."

"What am I going to do with it?"

"What do you think you're going to do with it?"

Bob held the weapon in his hands. It felt cold and heavy. He decided that Jan had gone off the deep end. There was no way that he was going to shoot Linda. Oh sure, Linda was annoying and they'd been fighting for months; plus he now despised her habits that he used to find cute when they first met ten years earlier, like her constant cleaning, her frumpy pajamas, her ugly face creams and foul smelling lotions, but that was a far cry from murder.

"You expect me to just walk into our apartment and shoot her?" he asked as he placed the gun on the night table.

"Of course not," she said, taking a sip from his water bottle, "you wait for her to fall asleep, and then you shoot her."

"Won't that make a lot of noise?"

"You put a pillow around the gun; it'll act as a silencer."

"Where'd you see that, on some TV show?"

"It doesn't matter where I saw it. I know it'll work."

Bob sat up and leaned against the bed board. "Okay, for the sake of argument, let's say it does, then what?"

"Then you open the window in your bedroom, the one you said faces the fire escape."

"I have a gate on it."

"You unlock the gate," she said, slitting her eyes, "and then you call the police."

"Aren't you leaving something out?"

"What?"

"I have to get rid of my clothes and gloves. They'll have gun powder residue on them."

"Where'd you hear that?"

"You're not the only one who watches TV."

She sniffed. "Okay, fine. Then you call the cops and tell them that you found her dead."

"Just like that?"

"Yeah. Then you and I live happily ever after."

"I don't want to go to jail."

"Who said anything about jail? You tell the cops that you came home and found her dead. Who's going to know the difference?"

"I have to think about it."

"Take the gun with you and don't think about it too much; just do it."

The next day at work, Bob did nothing but think about it. He sat in his cubicle, and stared off into space. His supervisor stopped by and told Bob to get back to work, that the company's new line of software products wouldn't sell itself. After the boss walked away Bob gazed at his computer screen, but it all seemed like a surreal jumble of names and numbers. Bob had never killed anyone before. The idea of killing his wife seemed terrifying. It was one thing to not like her, even, at times, to hate her, but to shoot her?

That night back at his apartment, he watched Linda sitting across the dinner table eating some spaghetti. She made a really irritating noise every time she sucked another strand into her mouth. Afterwards, Bob watched her clean off the table, rinse the dishes, and put them in the dishwasher.

"What is it?" asked Linda, after she sat down on the couch in the living room. "You're staring at me."

"I'm sorry."

"I'm not used to it. Lately, you've been ignoring me."

"I've had a lot on my mind," said Bob, as he sat down on a chair opposite her.

She picked up a magazine and opened it. "I hardly see you lately, with all that overtime you've been putting in at the office."

"Um, yeah." That "overtime" was named Jan, he thought.

Later in bed, Bob watched Linda as she slept, and tried to picture how the whole thing would go down. After a few minutes, he went to the window, unlocked the gate, slid it to the side and opened the window. Linda yawned and rubbed her eyes.

"What're you doing?" she asked, "it's freezing in here."

"I just wanted to get some air."

"Close the window and go to bed."

Bob closed the window and climbed back into bed, but it took a long time for him to fall asleep.

A couple of days later, Bob was back at the motel with Jan. Though they were in a different room than they had been before, it looked exactly alike, down to the badly painted Paris street scene on the wall. After they'd made love, Jan pulled away and said:

"So, what's going on with you and the wife?"

"Can you define, 'Going on?'"

"When are you going to do it? And don't ask me what I mean by 'it.'"

"I'm working my way up to it."

"And when do you think you'll be able to do it?"

"I—I'm not sure."

"You're really giving me a lot of confidence here."

"Be patient."

"Like hell I will. I need you to do this ASAP. I'm not getting any younger. Maybe this will help," said Jan, "if you don't do it within the next two weeks, I'm walking."

"What?"

"If you don't kill her in the next fourteen days, we're history." Jan got out of bed and began dressing. "Oh, and just so you know I'm serious, I don't want to see you again till you whack her."

During the next few days Bob pondered his options. He had to admit that he was in love with Jan. He wanted to be with her, and to be free of his wife. In the nights that followed he tried a couple of dry runs. In the middle of the night he got out of bed and took his pillow, brought it over to his sleeping wife, put his finger against it, and made a 'bang' noise, like little kids do when they play cowboys and Indians. Then he got back into bed.

On another night he decided to rehearse using the real gun. He got out of bed, retrieved the gun from a locked box where he'd hidden it, and stuck it into a pillow. Then he went over to his sleeping wife and whispered, "Kapow." Afterwards, he put the gun back in its hiding place and went to bed. Only now he found it difficult to get to sleep. He was having trouble getting from the practice sessions to actually doing it for real. His hand had shaken and he found the whole thing deeply disturbing. The prospect of losing Jan weighed heavily on him. Maybe if he gave it another day or two he could actually go through with it.

The next day, at his job, all Bob could think about were two things. Killing his wife, and Jan. Jan was the best lover he'd ever had. They'd been seeing each other for six months, and every time felt like the first time. With Linda it was like going through the motions. The killing would be just one shot at close range. He couldn't miss. Then he'd have to get rid of the gun. Jan hadn't mentioned that part, but it would be easy enough to do. He could even bury it in the park. He felt himself starting to feel more at ease about the whole idea. Maybe it was just a matter of getting used to it.

At lunch, Bob unwrapped a cheese sandwich Linda had made for him and bit into it. He noticed his co-worker Mike in the next cubicle drinking a can of soda and reading the afternoon paper. Bob saw the headline and nearly choked. It read, "Husband Arrested In Wife's Murder." He started coughing and took a sip of bottled water. His co-worker looked up from reading and said, "You okay, Bob?"

"Yeah," said Bob, swallowing, "I'm fine."

"You look a little green."

"I'm fine. Uh, do you know anything about the cover story?"

"Huh?" said Mike, closing the paper and glancing at it. "Sure, it's been all over the news this week. Where've you been living, in a cave?"

"I haven't been following the news this week."

"Some guy killed his old lady and tried to make it look like an accident. The cops were suspicious from the beginning. When a wife dies, everyone figures it's the husband who did it. Who else would want to kill somebody's wife?"

"Uh, yeah."

"You sure you're all right? You look kind of pale."

"I'm okay. I think I'll just go to the men's room and wash my face."

Bob stumbled through the hallway, got to the men's room, went into a stall, and threw up. Afterward, he leaned against the wall and took a few deep breaths.

After work, Bob went straight home. Linda wasn't there yet. He went to his hiding place, opened the locked box, removed the gun and left the apartment. He walked a few blocks to the river, up to the water's edge, threw the gun as far as he could, and watched it vanish beneath the waves.

On the way back to his apartment he thought the whole situation over again. Yes, he and Linda had their problems, there was no denying that. But he knew that he couldn't kill her. And as far as the money went, was a hundred thousand dollars' worth walking around with the guilt of having murdered someone? Not to mention the possibility of going to jail for life, or even getting a lethal injection? He decided that it wasn't. He would suggest to Linda that they see a marriage counselor. If she agreed, he would give it his best try. He'd stop seeing Jan. If things didn't work out with Linda, he'd get a divorce, just like many people do when they have problems in their marriage that they can't solve.

The more he went over it all, the better he felt. The idea of staying with Jan was crazy. Any woman who could encourage him to murder his wife could never be trusted. And speaking of trust, if he had gone along with her scheme, then she'd always know his secret. Suppose that in a couple of years they broke up, she could blackmail him, or worse, turn him in to the cops. He decided that he was making the right decision on every front. He'd call her tomorrow, ask to meet her, tell her he just couldn't go through with it. Then it would be over. Bob took a deep breath. He felt as if a great weight had been lifted from his shoulders.

Instead of going directly back to his apartment, he stopped at the deli across the street and brought a bouquet of daisies for Linda. He couldn't remember the last time he'd gotten her flowers. Bob walked into his apartment, put the flowers behind his back and called out, "Linda, it's me." When he got no answer, he walked to the bedroom and opened the door. He saw Jan holding a gun and standing over Linda, who lay on the floor, bloody and unmoving.

"What have you done?" asked Bob.

"I knew you didn't have the guts to do it, so I had to take matters into my own hands."

"But I'd changed my mind…."

"Well, change it back, dear."

"How did you get into the apartment?"

"I told Linda I was a co-worker of yours; she let me right in. Now, my love, unlock the gate to the fire escape, and open the window. And after you've done that, be a doll, and call the police."

The Outbursts of Everett True

THE SOMERSET WONDER

by Ron Goulart

Less than five minutes after the elephant halted the train, an attempt was made on Harry Challenge's life. That was late on the misty afternoon of Sunday, April 29, 1900.

He'd been sharing a table in the moderately swaying dining car with his magician friend, the Great Lorenzo. A lean, clean shaven man in his early thirties, Harry was in a downcast mood. The reason for that was the neatly folded cablegram in the breast pocket of his conservative dark suit.

It had reached him at his London hotel late on Saturday and read:

> Dear Son: Your nitwit reporter ladyfriend has disappeared. Get yourself to the village of Dimchester in Somerset. *The New York Enquirer,* that yellow rag she works for, is paying us a hell of a lot more than Jennie Barr is worth to find her. So go find her. Your devoted father, the Challenge International Detective Agency.

"I have never claimed," the portly magician was saying, "to be more than the world's most gifted illusionist, Harry. However, from time to time, it is true that I am visited with what might be termed visions, glimpses of what is going on elsewhere or portents of the impending future."

"Yep, I know that." Harry frowned. "And those visions that you suffer from have helped me in the past." Leaning forward, he rested both elbows on the crisp white tablecloth. "That's why I'm asking you to see what you can come up with about Jennie. She's been missing for close to three days and—"

"Alas, my boy, as I've explained before," cut in Lorenzo as he tugged at his ample side whiskers, "I have no control over this particular gift. The visions strike without warning. I can't summon them at—Yow!" His face suddenly went pale, he dropped his fork, doubled slightly and clutched at his ample middle.

The glasses and the silver on their table rattled as the train went chuffing around a bend. Outside the mist was growing thicker, masking the English countryside and the woodlands they were rushing through.

"Something?" asked Harry. "Or is it just indigestion? Since you've knocked off two éclairs and a fairy cake, it—"

Lorenzo, slowly, straightened up. His plump face was pale, dotted with perspiration, and this voice thin and a bit shaky. "Jennie is sitting next to a massive black safe. She's tied in a clawfooted chair, also gagged…it looked like they used a paisley scarf for that." Sighing, the magician leaned back in his chair. "That vision just hit, unbidden. At any rate, Harry, we now know the girl is still alive and in relatively good shape."

"Any idea where she is?"

The Great Lorenzo, forlornly, shook his head. "The majority of my glimpses don't come equipped with street addresses," he explained. "If I were to hazard a guess, however, I'd say she's being held somewhere in the vicinity of Dimchester. Since we'll be arriving in that benighted hamlet in…" From the watch pocket of his checkered silk vest he drew out a fat gold watch. "…in roughly ten minutes. I suggest you commence your search there."

"That's where I'm figuring to start anyway, Lorenzo," Harry pointed out. "Her editor, since Jennie's extremely independent, only knew that she came to Dimchester, chasing an important story. But he had no details. It'd be helpful if your next vision could provide a few more specifics."

"You're the detective," reminded the magician. "I have offered you, in my modest opinion, a helpful, a very helpful, hint. It is now up to you to exercise your considerable gift for ratiocination to find the poor lass."

"You're right, yeah." Harry extracted a thin black cigar from his case. "Worrying about her has made me a shade surly. Excuse it." He lit the cigar with a wax match. "Since your visions are usually damned reliable, we can be sure she's alive. That's good."

"Exactly. So now you can cease moping and concentrate on finding Jennie," said Lorenzo as he materialized another chocolate éclair out of the air. "And I can devote my evening not to commiserating with you over the temporary loss of your sweetheart but to planning my upcoming magic presentation at—"

"Jennie and I aren't exactly sweethearts, Lorenzo," he told him. "We like each other, sure, and we've spent quite a bit of time together. Since she covers unusual international stories for her newspaper and I specialize in cases with a supernatural element, that means we're going to coincide on—"

"Balderdash," observed the Great Lorenzo, taking an ambitious bite out of the latest pastry. "You two babes in the woods are a love match if ever I—"

"Get back," advised Harry, "to thinking about the magic show you're going to stage in Dimchester on May first."

"I'm not at all certain, you know, if the simple rustics who reside in and around Dimchester are anywhere near sophisticated enough to appreciate my performance, which has awed the crowned heads of Europe and many of the great minds of the Nineteenth Century." He took another bite of the éclair. "Yet, since I've been invited and paid a princely sum—princely, yet perhaps not anywhere near my true worth—to stage my Amazing Hour of Magic & Mystery at Tuesday's May Day Fête, I shall, seasoned trouper that I am, do my best."

"It was a fortunate coincidence that I'm heading for Dimchester, too, and we wound up on the same train." Harry exhaled smoke.

Lorenzo stroked his grizzled sideburns. "Perhaps, my boy," he observed quietly, "it is not a coincidence at all but, rather, the inexplicable doings of the fates who weave our—"

The train car suddenly stopped with a great series of grinding thumps. Harry's wine glass hopped free of their table, hitting the floor and splashing red as it turned into glistening fragments.

The misted windows rattled, silverware fell from surrounding tables. Diners shouted, gasped, pushed back in their chairs.

The door at the end of the dining car was yanked open and a capless conductor came stumbling in. "We nearly collided with an elephant," he said, one hand to his temple. "That's highly unusual in these parts."

The clowns came charging into the halted dining car as a dozen or so of the patrons were hurrying out to take a look at the elephant, who could be heard trumpeting angrily out in the fading afternoon.

There were three clowns and, although of varying sizes and shapes, they were all identically costumed. Each clown wore a small yellow bowler hat atop a luxuriant carrot-colored fight wig, a bulbous crimson nose, blue and gold polka dot pantaloons and an oversized purple peacoat festooned with six huge silver buttons. Two of them carried pistols and the third a hand-axe.

Lorenzo and Harry had remained at their table. "More strays from the circus that's playing Dimchester during the May Day festivities?" mused the portly magician.

"I doubt they're employed by the employers of the strayed elephant." Harry, casually, slid his hand into his coat. "Although they may be the ones who conveyed him onto the tracks to halt our train."

"Meaning that they, despite their outwardly jovial appearance, are up to no good."

The leanest clown was about ten feet away from them. Impatient, he shoved aside a heavyset, white-moustached and deeply tanned gentleman who might have served as an Army colonel in India earlier in life.

"I say, old fellow," the gentleman protested as he slammed against an abandoned table and sent the flower vase to the carpeted floor, "that's hardly sporting."

"Hard cheese, gov," replied the spurious clown. "You there with the fat bloke, are you "'Arry Challenge?"

"Fat, sir?" cried out the Great Lorenzo as he assumed an affronted look. "Fat, am I?"

While the armed clown's attention was turned toward the magician, Harry yanked his .38 revolver from his shoulder holster and shot the intruder in the pantaloons before he could aim his pistol at the detective.

"I am Harry Challenge, yeah," he answered, dodging to his left and ducking low.

As the initial red-nosed clown hopped about on the leg that wasn't bleeding, he yelled, "Foul, 'at's a blinking foul."

"I say," said the gentleman with the white moustache, "that was hardly sporting, old man. This clownish chap had hardly a chance to aim before you potted him. When two gentlemen are dueling, it's..."

"Shut your bloody gob," advised the second clown, who grabbed the colonel and, using him as a shield, took a shot at Harry.

Harry, however, was no longer where he had been seconds earlier and the slug missed him and went smashing out through a window beyond their table. That let in a grey swirl of chill, late afternoon mist.

Lorenzo, who was ducked down behind a tipped-over table said, "Prepare for another diversion, Harry."

From the floor of the dining car came rising a thick plume of deeply green smoke. It swiftly grew into an immense swirling cloud and engulfed two of the clowns and the protesting colonel.

The first clown was now, from the sound of him, lying flat out on the carpeting, kicking in pain, howling and cursing.

The second clown, also lost in the green mist, had decided to fire his weapon at random. "Your days are numbered, Challenge, and…Awk!"

Harry had ducked low, moved up close to the man and, making a shrewd guess as to the location, delivered a forceful kick to his groin. This clown now commenced howling and lamenting his fate in a high-pitched voice.

Harry sprinted clear of the green cloud in time to see the third clown, the one with the hand-axe, dive out of the dining car and off the halted train. "Look after these buffoons, Lorenzo," he called. "I'll catch the other one."

The escaping clown was running, as best he could in his baggy pantaloons and large floppy shoes, up toward the head of the train.

Beyond him Harry could see, blurred by the mist, a group of men with ropes, nets and pikes urging the annoyed Indian elephant to leave the train tracks and move into the woodlands that constituted the outskirts of the town of Dimchester.

The fleeing clown suddenly stopped, spun around and raised the axe to hurl it at Harry. "This'll fix you, you blooming toff."

'Not so fast, old chap." From out of the mist above him swooped a large muscular man. He was clad in a dark-colored cable-stitch sweater, white riding breeches and highly-polished black boots. His curly blond hair was worn long and the upper part of his face was hidden by a mask of black silk.

He appeared to be flying and he reached down to take hold of the startled clown by the back of his jacket.

Effortlessly, he lifted the man completely off the ground, rising up at least ten feet with him. "Let this be a lesson to you, my good man," he said in his deep, booming voice and dropped the clown.

One of the conductors was staring up at the masked man. "Blimey," he exclaimed, "if it ain't the Wonder!"

When the clown landed about two yards from Harry, his red nose popped free and went bouncing away on the grass.

The constable of Dimchester was a middle-sized and chiefly bald man of fifty. Leaning with his elbow against the mantel of the small fireplace in the parlor of his overly cozy cottage on the town square, he was saying, "I am, Mr. Challenge, a great admirer of yours. I've clipped newspaper accounts of your investigative accomplishments for several years. I especially enjoy those written by that daring young reporter, Jennie Barr, and I—"

"That's why I'm here." Harry was sitting on the edge of a purplish Morris chair. "Jennie disappeared from your town three days ago and—"

"I was fully aware that the poor girl had vanished." Constable Mulliner's pipe went out again and he applied another match to the tobacco in the bowl. "It troubles me greatly that my men and I haven't been able, after being contacted by her New York editors, to find a trace of her."

"Have you learned anything?"

Mulliner took two puffs of his pipe. "She left the Cheshire Cat Inn, where I understand you're also staying, at nine in the morning on Wednesday last. Although she told old Googins the innkeeper that she'd be back in time for lunch, she never returned. We have, alas, found no one who saw her after she'd left on that fateful morning."

"You have any idea what sort of a story Jennie Barr was here working on?"

The constable shook his head. "If the young woman confided in anyone," he replied, "we have been unable to find that person. I had hoped, since they ply the same trade, that Denis Farrington might have some notion of what the girl was up to, but he—"

"Denis Farrington?" Harry straightened in his chair.

"Yes, he's the editor and chief reporter of the *Dimchester Weekly Observer*. Is that a clue?"

Farrington, Harry was fairly certain, was a friend of the missing reporter. "Nope, I just had the notion I'd heard the name before."

"Farrington's quite well-known throughout Somerset." Leaving the area of the fireplace, Constable Mulliner settled into a bentwood rocker facing the detective. "These fellows who tried to do you in earlier today—and I believe we're safe in saying that they stole the elephant from the circus that's appearing in town in order to use it to halt the train and afford them an opportunity to assault you. Would it be safe to conclude, Mr. Challenge, that these fellows wanted to prevent you from finding Jennie Barr?"

"It would, yes."

"Do you think your traveling companion, Mr. Lorenzo, will be able to find out—"

"He prefers to be called the Great Lorenzo." Harry lit a new thin black cheroot. "He's very good at finding out things, which is why I sent him over to talk to the two clown impersonators."

"He won't use American means of inquiry on them, I trust. The third degree I believe you call it over there," said the constable. "We have a very conservative town council and, while I wish to be helpful to you, I wouldn't—"

"He won't lay a hand on them," promised Harry, exhaling smoke. "He may also want to drop in at the infirmary to talk with the clown with the broken leg."

Mulliner said, "As soon as Dr. Needham gives his permission."

Harry took a slow drag on his cigar. "Now tell me about the Wonder."

The constable gave a negative shake of his hand. "Merely an old wives' tale," he assured Harry. "A bit of latter day folklore that—"

"I saw him," reminded Harry. "He flew by, scooped up the clown and rose into the air with him. Then he dropped him. The Wonder is a very palpable piece of folklore."

"I've never seen this wonderful chap myself," said the constable, whose pipe yet again ceased function. "I venture to say, however, that his alleged exploits—carrying residents out of a burning building, lifting carts out of the mud, thrashing bullies and all the rest—have been greatly exaggerated."

"How long has he been operating, greatly exaggerated or not, in the vicinity of Dimchester?"

Constable Mulliner considered. "Nearly two months, I calculate," he answered. "At least that's about when I started hearing tales about him."

"You have any idea as to who he is?"

"Never having seen the Wonder, I am unable to form any opinions as to his identity," the local lawman said. "In my opinion he's nothing more than a prankster bent on gulling the simpler denizens of the area."

"I understand he helped get the elephant clear of the train tracks."

"Another embroidery of the truth."

Harry leaned back in his chair. "If Jennie got wind of the Somerset Wonder, she'd come here to find out about him. It's her sort of yarn and something she specializes in writing about for the *New York Enquirer*."

"Can her attempting to learn something about the Wonder have anything to do with her being kidnapped?"

"We don't know she's been kidnapped or what she was digging into." Harry stood. "Think I'll get over to the jail to find out what, if anything, the Great Lorenzo has—"

The brass knocker on the constable's front door was vigorously activated.

A moment later the magician came hurrying into the parlor. He looked a shade winded. "Take a gander, my boy, at this poster," he said. "I noticed it on a siding whilst I was trudging back from the local hoosegow." He unfurled the large bright poster.

Sensational Appearance of
World Famed Soprano
in an
EXCITING RECITAL
of Opera Favorites!
LILY HOPE in Person!
3 Days Only at the Town Hall.
May 1 to May 3.
Do Not Miss This Tremendous Event!!

"Would this be a clue?" inquired Mulliner.

In addition to being a passable singer, Lily Hope was also a very successful international spy. Harry wondered what in the devil she was doing in Dimchester. "Actually no. It's only that both Lorenzo and I are devoted admirers of the lady's golden voice."

"Indeed, yes," seconded the plump magician. "She puts the nightingale to shame."

The constable asked Lorenzo, "Did you find out anything from the prisoners?"

"Not much I fear," he lied. "I concluded that these fellows are merely thugs for hire, imported from London to lie in wait for my dear friend, Harry Challenge, and incapacitate him."

"For what purpose?"

"Their anonymous employer didn't see fit, it seems, to share his motives with them," answered the magician. "All they know is that they were hired to prevent him from reaching town."

"Wonder why people want to keep me away from here," said Harry.

Lorenzo faced Harry, his back to the constable. "We shall have to find out, my boy." He winked and mouthed the words, "We'll talk later."

Rewinding his scarf around his neck, the Great Lorenzo said, "I appreciate your accompanying me to the Barksdale Mansion, Harry. A walking companion on a dismal foggy night such as—"

"I'm not interested all that much in tagging along while you take a look at where you'll be putting on your magic show come Tuesday," he told his friend. "What I want to know is what, if anything, you learned from those two louts who attempted to knock me off."

"That is exactly what I intend to tell you, my boy," said the magician. "I didn't think it prudent to discuss the matter while under the eye of the constable."

Impatiently, Harry requested, "So tell me now. Did either of them know where Jennie—"

"Afraid not," answered Lorenzo. "The method of interviewing I utilized when I was alone with each of these miscreants was tried and true as well as reliable." Extracting his gold watch from the pocket of his vest, he swung it from side to side a few times.

"I know you're a pretty fair hypnotist. That's why I suggested that you—"

"Pretty fair? I happen to be, and this was confirmed at the most recent meeting of the International Hypnotists Guild, I happen to be one of the most gifted hypnotists on the face of the Earth."

"When you hypnotized these guys, you got nothing about Jennie's whereabouts?"

The two of them reached the northern end of town and started along the foggy forest trail that led to the mansion of Sir Danvers Barksdale, the millionaire who'd hired the Great Lorenzo to stage his magic show at his mansion as part of the upcoming town-wide May Day festivities.

"They could not provide any information about your feisty sweetheart's current location, Harry," said the magician. "They were, however, able to tell me who hired them to assist you in shuffling off to oblivion and why."

"You showed me the poster announcing Lily Hope's presence in Dimchester," said Harry as the night woods closed in around them. "So I assume she's involved."

"Undoubtedly, although neither of them had any contact with the lady spy," explained the portly magician. "What they both confessed, when under my expertly applied hypnotic spell, was that an extremely tall man hired them to make certain you'd never arrive here. An extremely tall man, excessively bald and sporting an obvious glass eye."

"Oskar Tortuga," said Harry. "Lily's bodyguard and go-between."

"That was my conclusion, yes."

Off in the misty dark an owl hooted.

"Okay, so Lily doesn't want me in the vicinity," Harry said slowly. "That means she's here for something besides singing off key at the town hall. What did your informants say?"

"Only that Tortuga hinted you represented competition."

"And do Lily and her toady consider Jennie competition, too?"

"Very likely, Harry, but our erstwhile clowns had nothing to do with the lass's vanishing."

"I'll add Lily to my list of folks to call on tomorrow."

"This flying man you claim to have encountered," said the magician. "What do you think is the cause of him?"

"Well, Lorenzo, he could be a uniquely gifted rustic who's succeeded in teaching himself to fly, lift elephants and perform other impressive chores," replied Harry. "Or he might be the result of some pioneering scientific experiment."

The Great Lorenzo nodded. "Our dear Lily is well-known for supplying pilfered plans and formulas pertaining to assorted engines of war to sundry foreign powers," he said. "A process, if such there is, for turning everyday lads into flying strongmen would be extremely interesting to many a belligerent nation."

"Yep, and Lily has worked for quite a few war-minded countries," he said. "It's also possible, Lorenzo, that Jennie got wind of this Somerset Wonder, came here to look into the story and—"

Chesty barking had started up ahead, along with the sound of more than one running dog.

"We must be near the mansion," suggested Lorenzo, "and Sir Danvers has let loose the hounds."

There were three substantial dogs, two mastiffs and a German shepherd. They came galloping out of the night mist. Halting a few yards from Harry and the magician, they stood, wide-legged, and snarled.

"I've had notable luck hypnotizing cows and horses," said the Great Lorenzo as he extracted his gold watch from its pocket. "Not much with hounds, particularly with those intent on sinking their teeth into me."

Harry drew his .38 revolver out of his shoulder holster. "We'll have more luck trying to dissuade them with this."

"As an animal lover, Harry, I'd hate to be a party to slaughtering these potentially noble creatures."

The dogs, back hair bristling, were inching closer, growling deep inside.

"I'm, basically, fond of animals, too," Harry assured him. "Less fond of being gobbled up by three ferocious hounds. Initially, I'll just fire over their heads to scare them off."

"It occurs to me that green smoke might be equally efficacious in frightening them away," said the magician as he reached into his coat pocket. "Fortunately, I usually carry a supply of—"

"No need for violence, gentlemen." The leafy branches of the trees on their right rustled. The Wonder dropped to the ground a few feet behind the angry snarling dogs. "I'll handle these fellows."

"This, I take it," said Lorenzo, "is the Wonder that you alluded to earlier."

"The same, yeah."

The trio of hounds turned to bark at the blond man who'd dropped from above.

"Sit," he ordered.

Making a whimpering noise, one of the mastiffs obliged immediately. The other mastiff, after wagging his tail to and fro twice, also sat. The German shepherd, however, leaped at the Wonder.

While the growling animal was still in midair, the Wonder took two swift steps forward to deliver a single blow to its forehead.

Yelping once, the dog fell to the ground unconscious.

"Go back to your kennel," suggested the Wonder in a deep, persuasive voice.

The two mastiffs, deciding that this was sound advice, went padding away and were soon swallowed by the mist.

"You chaps can continue on in safety."

Putting his gun away, Harry asked, "What do you know about Jennie Barr?"

The Wonder hesitated for a few seconds before shaking his head. Crouching, he then leaped upward. He continued to ascend, rose up above the trees and then went flying away.

"Very impressive," observed Lorenzo.

"Apparently the dogs share your view."

"I am wondering, though, why he was wearing a wig."

"What in the bloody hell have you fools done to Satan?" A fat, red-faced man in a Norfolk jacket and plus fours was stomping toward them along the woodland trail. Cradled in his arms was a bright new shotgun.

"A more applicable question," suggested the magician, "is what was your dog planning to do to us."

"Stuff and nonsense. Satan happens to be a very valuable dog, sir, and we'll just see what good your pathetic sophistry does you at the next assizes. I am noted hereabouts for prosecuting poachers to the full—"

"This is the Great Lorenzo," cut in Harry. "If under all that bluster you happen to be Sir Danvers Barksdale, you should have been expecting him and not sending a batch of mean-minded hounds to—"

"I can assure you, young man, that this dog is far more important to me than a carnival trickster that my giddy wife browbeat me into hiring for the sole purpose of mystifying the hordes of halfwits and yahoos who constitute our neighbors."

"In that case, Sir Danvers," said the angry Lorenzo, "we can mutually cancel Tuesday's scheduled performance of my justly world-famed magic extravaganza. And you have my permission to take a—"

"Pay no attention to Danvers." A slim blonde woman of about thirty-five, wearing a dark velvet cloak, had appeared out of the mist. "You're more than welcome and we feel honored to have a magician of the caliber of the Great Lorenzo entertain at Barksdale Mansion."

"A magician of his caliber," said Sir Danvers loudly, "has nearly murdered poor Satan, Florence."

Lady Barksdale said, "The pup's only dazed and, look, he's already getting to his feet. I don't blame the Great Lorenzo for administering a much needed clout to him."

"It was not I, dear lady, who felled the beast," the magician informed Barksdale's much younger wife. "No, a local fellow who is known, I believe, as the Somerset Wonder, dispatched Satan before he had a chance to gnaw on us."

Sir Danvers lowered his shotgun. "The Wonder was here? You actually saw the bloke?"

"We most certainly did," answered Lorenzo. "Now then, what is to be the upshot of this unpleasant encounter? Am I to assume that the multitudes of Dimchester citizens who've been eagerly anticipating the advent of what many astute observers truly believe to be the greatest magic show in the world are to be disappointed? Disappointed to the extent of turning against the entire Barksdale clan and possibly marching through the quaint streets of the town brandishing blazing torches and—"

"Don't be silly," cut in Lady Barksdale. "You most certainly shall appear as scheduled, sir. Come up to the house." She made a come-with-me gesture with her right hand. "And bring your friend."

"This is Harry Challenge." Lorenzo gestured in the detective's direction.

Sir Danvers took a sudden step backwards, nearly stumbling over his still somewhat dazed dog. "Harry Challenge of the Challenge International Detective Agency?"

"Yes, I happen to be that Harry Challenge," confirmed Harry.

"What a shame our son is away for the day," said the blonde women. "Roger is very interested in detective work and he's followed your career with keen interest, Mr. Challenge."

"Allow me to apologize for this unfortunate little misunderstanding," said Sir Danvers, failing to sound completely convincing. "Do come up to the house."

"Such has been my intention all along," Lorenzo told him.

Monday morning was blustery and the hanging sign over the entrance of the Cheshire Cat was creaking enthusiastically as Harry, alone, emerged from the inn.

His initial destination was the office of the Dimchester Weekly Observer some six blocks away. The newspaper was housed in a small Tudor-style building halfway down a quirky cobblestone lane.

Displayed in the wide front window was the front page of the latest edition. There were three 16-point headlines that caught Harry's attention. Famed American Reporter Disappears, Mystery Man Rescues Noted American Detective, and Local Eccentric Scientist Still Missing. The stories about Jennie, himself, and the Somerset Wonder told Harry nothing new. The piece dealing with the missing scientist he found more informative. A Dr. Spartacus Donne, noted for his unorthodox researches in the fields of nutrition and physical fitness, had vanished from his woodland cottage, which also served as a laboratory, the day after Jennie had gone missing.

"Maybe there's a link," Harry said to himself and entered the newspaper office.

The place smelled strongly of newsprint and black ink and from the small workroom beyond the office came the sound of a press at work.

Seated at the oak desk at the left of the office was a tall, handsome, dark-haired man of about forty. "I say," he said, half rising from his chair, "you're Harry Challenge, aren't you? What a coincidence, since there's a story pertaining to you in this week's—"

"Not much of a coincidence. I came to see you because I'm looking for Jennie Barr," he told the editor. "As I recall you're a friend of hers who met her while you were working on a London daily about three years ago."

"Two and a half years ago, old boy," corrected Denis Farrington. "I was, as you may know, a brief and unsuccessful suitor of that brilliant young lady. It's always been my suspicion that her fondness for you was the chief reason I never—"

"You've kept in touch with Jennie."

"I have. Our friendship continues."

Harry straddled a straight-back chair and faced the editor. "Are you the one who suggested she come to Dimchester?"

"Afraid I am, Challenge," he admitted. "My motives were fairly honest and I didn't invite Jennie simply because I wanted to see her again."

"No, I imagine you told her all about the Somerset Wonder."

"Yes, because it struck me as something ideally suited to her, the very sort of unusual, possibly supernatural, phenomenon that she writes about so well in the pages of the *New York Inquirer*."

"And she was investigating the Wonder when she disappeared?"

"She was, Challenge. We had dinner the night before and Jennie implied she had unearthed a very promising lead."

"Which was?"

He gave a forlorn shake of his head. "I'm not certain, since she didn't confide any details in me," Farrington said. "I do know that one of the people she planned to call on the next day was Dr. Donne."

"The guy who disappeared the day after she did."

"I've encountered Donne often since resettling in Dimchester," said the editor. "I consider the chap nothing more than a harmless loon. Jennie, obviously, thought otherwise."

Taking a thin cigar out of his case, Harry lit it. "Do you know who the Wonder is?"

"I've never actually seen him and thus far none of the witnesses to his good deeds has been armed with a camera."

"But that is what the guy's up to, doing good deeds and helping people out of trouble?"

The other man nodded. "I don't doubt the chap's motives," he said. "He is, or rather I assume he somehow became, what Bernard Shaw borrowing from the German philosophers, would call a superman."

After exhaling smoke, Harry asked, "Do you know who Lily Hope is?"

"Oh, yes. She's earned quite a sizeable reputation with the espionage activities. Her Majesty's Secret Service has accumulated quite a dossier on the lady, although they have thus far been unable to prove a case against her."

"It's quite possible that Lily's here searching for the secret of the Somerset Wonder," suggested Harry, "and that she may be involved in what's happened to Jennie."

"That hadn't occurred to me, Challenge."

"Okay, you're fond of Jennie and you've been on the scene since the day she disappeared," Harry said. "Where do you think she might be?"

"That's what's so annoying," said the editor. "I've gotten nowhere. I've always considered myself a capable reporter, yet I've been unable to turn up a single clue."

Harry rose up. "I intend to find her," he said. "So if you learn anything, I'd appreciate—"

"The fact that you're searching for Jennie has already prompted someone, possible Lily Hope, to try to kill you," reminded Farrington. "You'd best be deucedly careful from here on out, old man."

"I almost always am," Harry told him.

Harry took a second sip of his glass of dark ale and decided it was as foul-tasting as the first. Setting the glass on the rutted wooden table, he leaned forward again and, cautiously, looked out the narrow stained window of the smoky pub.

Across the way a closed carriage was pulling up at the rear entrance of Town Hall. A moment later, the dark-haired Lily Hope emerged from the building and walked toward the waiting carriage. Her scarlet cloak was not completely closed and the bodice portion of her low-cut off-white gown briefly showed.

"Yep, Lily has definitely gained a few pounds since last we met," he decided, leaving his table and crossing to the exit.

He stood just inside the doorway until her carriage went rolling away, heading uphill. Then he unobtrusively stepped out into the waning afternoon.

Parked in front of the public house was the bicycle Harry'd rented earlier in the day. He had successfully tailed the international lady spy from her hotel to her rehearsal. Now he was interested in learning where she headed next.

The dark conveyance, driven by her associate, the elongated Tortuga, turned onto a cobblestone street that led out of Dimchester. Harry followed at a distance and, when he saw Lily head along the narrow road leading to Barksdale's mansion, he parked the bicycle in among the stately oaks and continued on foot shielded by trees.

By the time he reached the vicinity of the sprawling mansion, the carriage was parked to the rear of the place. Lily, arms folded beneath her breasts, was standing on the flagstones nearby and seemingly arguing with Tortuga. He was scowling down at her, tapping his blunt forefinger against his glass eye.

"Finish him...take care of him now!' Harry heard her say before she turned on her heel to go striding toward the house. She didn't, however, head for the front of the venerable place. She instead walked around to the back.

Harry, keeping hidden among the trees, followed her.

He heard the carriage depart, then, watching through the brush, he saw Lily pulling open an unpainted wooden door and start down a stone stairway.

Harry waited for close to five minutes before he left the protection of the woods to go sprinting across the twilight grounds to the door.

It wasn't a difficult lock to pick and Harry was in the dim-lit stone corridor quite soon and making his careful way downward.

As the Great Lorenzo, wearing his most impressive scarlet-lined cape, pushed open the weathered wooden door of the photography shop, the overhead bell produced a somewhat rusty tinkle.

The proprietor was seated on a not-quite-sturdy stool behind the counter. A gaunt grey-bearded man, he was bent forward and hand-tinting a photograph.

"I sincerely hope, sir, that you're daubing my photos with your paint box water colors," said the magician as he approached. "Your hand seems none too steady and, judging from the rainbow splotches on your old grey beard, you miss the target more than you hit it."

Looking up, the photographer set aside his brush and touched at his beard. "Absentmindedness is the cause of the condition of my whiskers, Mr. Lorenzo," he explained. "When I'm deeply involved in my work, I tend to wipe my brushes on my beard rather than pick up the piece of scrap muslin that my dear wife so—"

"A most touching account of a doting wife's devotion to art," cut in the portly magician. "However, I am here to pick up the two dozen six-by-nine copies of the photograph you took of me in my impressive magical attire. The very same outfit that prompted the usually taciturn Queen Victoria to cry out at a recent Command Performance, 'Hey, lordy momma, what a fine rig.'"

"Ah," said the gaunt proprietor with a sigh indicating moderate concern, "I'm a bit late, Mr. Lorenzo, because I promised young Roger Barksdale that I would have the hand-tinted photographic portraits him in his full Khyber Rifles uniform ready late this afternoon."

"I am presenting my justly renowned and totally mystifying magical extravaganza at the Barksdale Mansion on the morrow, which fact I made, I thought, overly clear to you," the Great Lorenzo, frowning deeply, reminded. "It is my custom to bestow suitably inscribed portraits of myself to the initial wave of the ladies who flock to the stage at the end of my performance."

"I'll definitely have the pictures ready tomorrow morning," the photographer promised. "Tell you what, Mr. Lorenzo, for no extra cost I'll hand-tint the entire batch for you."

"I don't wish to be tinted."

"My color method will definitely enhance the portraits," the shopkeeper assured him. "Here, just take a look at the splendid job I'm doing on this portrait of Roger Barksdale." He held up the eight by ten photographs he'd been working on.

Lorenzo glanced at the picture of the dark-haired, brightly uniformed young man. "The poor lad looks like someone a mortician has had his way with," he observed. "The coloring is gaudy and untrue to—Well, I'll be blessed. It's the Somerset Wonder."

"No, no, you're quite mistaken," the photographer told him. "I had the privilege of being a fascinated and enthusiastic observer when the Wonder saved the Wollter lad from drowning at the mill. He's much larger than Roger and has blond hair worn long in the manner of some artists and poets." He shook his head. "No, take the word of a longtime town resident, Mr. Lorenzo. No one who really knows Roger Barksdale would mistake that mild-mannered and polite young man for a dynamic outgoing chap like the Wonder." He produced an amused chuckling sound.

Lorenzo extracted the photo from the man's fingers, studied it more closely. "Why, to be sure, I now see my correction," he lied. "You're absolutely right about a long-time resident being the one qualified to know what's what." He took two steps back. "I'll call for my photographs tomorrow. I've just remembered a previous engagement."

He left the shop very rapidly.

For a dungeon, it was quite comfortable. Some time recently the large stone-walled room far below the ground had been renovated and, from the looks of the place, an expensive London-based decorator had gone to work.

There were too many armchairs, too many large historical paintings hanging on the walls, too many Persian rugs covering the flagstone floor. And the large black safe in the far corner was far too big for the room.

The food wasn't bad, either, although Jennie Barr thought there was too much mutton on the menu and the Cabernet they always sent with dinner was an inferior French import.

She had been, by her calculations, a prisoner down here for going on four days. This refurbished dungeon, Jennie was fairly certain, was beneath the mansion of Sir Danvers Barksdale. Her first day here, while she was slowly awakening from being waylaid and drugged on her way to interview Dr. Spartacus Donne, she had heard Sir Danvers's gruff, raspy voice cursing whoever it was who kidnapped her.

By the time she was fully awake, the millionaire was not in the room. She'd interviewed him three years ago when he was opening a new munitions plant in an outlying section of London.

Since that first day only a frail, wispy, and uncommunicative maid had ever visited Jennie's prison. There were two meals a day. The maid had untied Jennie and removed the gag before serving her first meal.

No one, not even the maid, had spoken to her since she'd been detained here.

"I'm pretty sure why I was abducted," she'd said to herself. "It must have something to do with my looking into this darned Wonder's career. Somebody doesn't want me to learn who he is or how he got to be what he is."

The trouble was, Jennie didn't know a heck of a lot. She'd written an article about Dr. Donne last year when he was the object of not one but two satirical drawings in *Punch* and she was aware that he claimed to be working on an elixir that would after only a few doses, convert an average mild-mannered youth into a superior fighting man. She had hoped to get Donne, who'd settled in Dimchester some months earlier, to discuss his process and confirm her suspicion that the Somerset Wonder was his handiwork.

A key turned in the lock of the thick oaken door of her dungeon suite.

Tossing her notebook on the bedside table, the slim auburn-haired reported moved a few steps nearer to the door.

Into the room stepped an attractive, slightly overweight woman in her late thirties. "Good afternoon, Jennie dear," she said, smiling from the threshold.

"Darned if it is isn't Lily Hope," Jennie said. "So you're the one behind my kidnapping."

"Think of it more as a temporary detention," said the singing spy. "Soon as my work in this backwater is completed, you'll be set free unharmed."

"And why am I being detained at all?"

"Your own fault," Lily told her. "You're much too much the Nosy Parker and we don't want you getting in our way."

"I have a hunch," said the reporter, "that Harry Challenge is going to come looking for me, Lil. He's always been able to throw a spanner into your schemes. I bet he'll do it again."

"Don't count on Harry," advised Lily. "If all goes well, he'll be out of the way before this day is over."

The oil in the bracket lamp on the grey stone wall gave off a sharp, sooty odor and a chill draft caused the weak flame to flicker. Harry, now ten minutes underground, paused to stand listening.

From a dozen yards further along the shadowy corridor came, faintly, the sound of two voices. Female voices.

Slowly and quietly, Harry eased forward. On his right as he descended, he passed the entrance, a dark, damp-smelling opening to another underground passway.

Up ahead a woman cried out, "Damn you, you impudent vixen!"

"That's Lily Hope," Harry realized and sprinted forward.

Next came the sound of an interrupted scream and a groan of pain. Then something heavy and wooden hit a floor. A short-lived sigh followed, and a muffled thud.

By the time of the thud, he was beside a thick wooden door on the left-hand side of the damp stone corridor. Cautiously, Harry tried the handle. The door was locked.

"Another test of my cracksman skills." He crouched to work on the lock.

All at once the heavy oaken door swung open outward.

He bounced upright, backpedaled, reaching for his shoulder holster.

"Harry, what a pleasant surprise," said Jennie Barr, smiling as she stepped into the corridor. "I imagine you're here to rescue me, but, see, I'm quite capable of looking after myself."

"Oh, so?" He let his gun slide back into its holster. "Then how come it's taken you four days to escape. Seems to me that if—"

"Didn't mean to damage your self esteem." Still smiling, she moved close to Harry, rose on tip toe to kiss him on the cheek. "Really, honestly, I do appreciate your taking the time to track me down. It shows that our friendship—"

"Your damned newspaper hired us to rescue you, Jen."

"Even so."

He asked, "What exactly happened to you?"

"Your dear friend, Lily Hope, the singing spy, had me abducted." She explained, pointing a thumb over her shoulder into the room where she'd been imprisoned. "While Lily was gloating over me just now, I managed to kick her in the shins, conk her with a chair, and lay her out on a very handsome Persian carpet. She's lying unconscious even as we speak, Harry dear."

"Might I escort you the hell out of here? Be a good idea to do that while she's still out cold."

"Yes, but let's truss her up and gag her," the pretty reporter suggested. "We can send somebody back to collect her later."

"Okay, but swiftly."

Jennie went back into the comfortably furnished cell. "In a while, Harry, I'll explain to you what this is all about," she promised as he followed her. "I'd appreciate it though, if you'd let me file my story before you go blurting out the details of—"

"C'mon, Jennie, you know I never blurt." He stopped next to the sprawled body of the unconscious spy. "Besides, I already know about the disappearance of Dr. Donne and Lily's attempts to learn the secret of the Somerset Wonder."

Kneeling to tie Lily with the ropes that had earlier been used on her, Jennie made an exasperated sound. "I am, Harry, as you know, quite fond of you," she said to him. "But, gosh, I do wish you weren't so darn smug at times."

Jennie took three more steps along the shadowy corridor, inhaled sharply, tightened her grip on Harry's arm, and halted. "Damn," she remarked.

"Exactly," agreed the detective.

Sir Danvers Barksdale had emerged from the side corridor a few yards in front of them. "Come along, my dear. You, too, Challenge old boy." The flickering lamplight reflected on the barrel of the shotgun he held pointed at them.

"Not only are you an accessory to kidnapping," Harry pointed out to the heavyset, flush-faced owner of Barksdale Mansion, "you can also be charged with attempted murder—mine—and conspiring to steal an elephant."

"Enough of your bloody nattering." Barksdale gestured with the shotgun barrel. "Be so kind, the both of you, as to trot along that corridor yonder. Do, please, be deuced fast about it."

"Any time that Harry Challenge appears on the scene," explained Jennie, "it is usually a sign that the jig is nigh to being up, Sir Danvers. Why not quit now while—"

"Being a gentleman, Miss Barr, shooting a woman would seriously upset me," the fat man told her. "However, I'll be damned well to do it should the pair of you not move and now."

They moved.

The crypt was thick with the scents of damp earth and ancient dust. About the size of a large parlor, the upper third of its venerable stone walls was above ground. Four stone coffins rested on low pedestals at the rear of the chamber. There was one small stained glass window on the wall opposite the three heavy wooden chairs occupied by Jennie, Harry, and Dr. Spartacus Donne. Rain was falling heavily in the fading day outside. The rising wind was slapping it against the multicolor chunks of ancient glass and the thick iron door at the head of the short flight of stone steps leading down into the dim lit room.

"No luck so far." Jennie was struggling against the ropes that held her bound to her chair. "How about you?"

Harry, a half dozen feet to her right, replied, "Lorenzo taught me some of his best escape tricks. I ought to be able to—"

"Hopeless, hopeless," lamented the lean rumpled scientist who was slumped in the chair next to the detective. "We'll never free ourselves from these infernal ropes. Our plight, if I may be permitted to observe, is hopeless. I have been held prisoner by these scoundrels for lo, these many long days and I fear I shan't be able to withhold my secret much longer."

"Three or four days," observed Jennie, pausing in her struggle with her ropes, "isn't exactly lo, these many days, doctor. Thus far, I notice, they haven't done you any physical harm."

"That's coming, miss. They've promised torture should I not confide," the inventor informed her. "When that death merchant Barksdale returns with Lily Hope—a gifted singer, yet, alas, an evil-hearted woman—they'll commence using physical persuasion to learn my method of creating an Ubermensch."

"How many of them have you created thus far?" asked the reporter.

"Just one."

"And who is he?"

Dr. Donne sighed. "I vowed not to reveal the true identity of the Somerset Wonder." He shook his head. "The young man feels that he can better carry on his noble deeds if no one is aware of his true identity." He sighed again. "Were I to reveal who he is, you would no doubt be struck by the irony of the situation. In fact, it is most unfortunate that—"

"My blooming patience has worn thin, Donne." Sir Danvers Barksdale came up through the entrance in the crypt floor that he had ushered Jennie and Harry up through a few hours earlier. He carried his shotgun tucked under one arm. "No more coddling, old chap. It'll be talk or torture hence forward."

Lily Hope climbed up into the stone room next. She had a sticking plaster on her right cheek, a dark bruise under her right eye. "There's no need to question Jennie Barr," she remarked. "As soon as this old fool provides the information we want, Danvers, we can shoot her." She moved closer to the bound reporter. "My associate, Tortuga, enjoys handling such chores, but this time I'll dispatch you myself."

"There's no need for that, Lily," put in Harry. "Once you swipe the information you want, you can—"

"Damn, man," shouted Barksdale. "We aren't here to bloody bargain. Both you meddlers will be shot and left here afterwards. Nobody ever comes near this old Barksdale family tomb. You can both rot away here in peace and quiet."

Lily moved closer to Jennie, easing into the space between her chair and Harry's. "I have never, I must admit, been able to understand why poor Harry finds you attractive. I've seen skinny, ragged urchins begging on the streets of London who're better looking than you." She lunged, slapped the auburn-haired reporter across the face and stepped back, nearly bumping into the seated detective.

Harry, who'd managed to, unnoticed, undo the ropes that held him jumped to his feet and grabbed the singer by both her arms. He spun her around to face the muttering Barksdale, using her as a shield.

"A most cowardly act, sir," accused Sir Danvers, "hiding behind a woman's skirts. Put her aside, you bounder."

"Skirt. Thanks for reminding me," said Harry as he let go of the spy's arms and slipped his left arm Gad, firmly around her waist. With his now free right hand, he reached down, lifted the hem of Lily Hope's long skirt. "Good, you're still wearing it strapped to your leg." His hand emerged hold a pearl-handled .22 pistol.

"Throw that bally weapon away," ordered Barksdale, swinging the barrel of his shotgun so that it was aimed directly at Harry and Lily. "I am, I assure you, deucedly fond of Lily—a damned handsome woman for her age, a top-hole spy, and a passable soprano. But I'll shoot through her to get at you."

"What do you mean for my age, you old halfwit?" demanded Lily, scowling. "I won't be thirty-five until next March."

"Abandon the gun, Challenge. I usually only count to three in situations like this, but since Lily is involved I'll count to ten before firing."

At that moment the heavy iron door of the ancient family crypt gave out a sudden resounding clang. Then it was torn off its rusty hinges and tossed away into the rain-swept dusk outside.

The Great Lorenzo, huh?" Jennie asked Harry.

"None other, I'd say."

Through the smoke came flying the Somerset Wonder. He landed, wide-legged, in front of Sir Danvers, yanking the shotgun from his grasp. He bent the barrel in half before flinging it aside.

The flung gun landed atop one of the stone coffins.

"So it is unfortunately true," said the Wonder forlornly. "I did not so much as suspect until Mr. Lorenzo shared his vision with me. Then I realized that my own father was involved in a foul scheme to steal Dr. Donne's secret in order to sell it to a foreign power."

"How dare you call me father, you long-haired blond buffoon?" asked the angry Barksdale.

The Somerset Wonder yanked off his wig, then his mask. "It is I, father," he said in a cold level voice. "I am the one known as the Somerset Wonder."

His father's face grew more crimson. "All I can say, young sir, is that you have disappointed me yet again," he told him. "You know blessed well that I wanted you to join me in the munitions trade eventually."

Harry, who'd just completed untying Jennie, suggested, "What say we fetch Constable Mulliner?"

"I fear we must," said young Barksdale.

The Great Lorenzo, hands clasped behind his broad back, was surveying the empty Town Hall stage. "A most fortunate turn of events, my boy," he remarked to Harry. "Since Lily Hope is now in the clutches of the constabulary and won't be able to stage her evenings of caterwauling here, this quaint old edifice is available. I'll be able to present my internationally renowned and respected magical extravaganza here instead of at the Barksdale Mansion."

Harry nodded. "Since Sir Danvers paid you in advance, you can hold on to that dough as well."

"All perfectly fair and legal." The portly magician commenced a slow circuit of the late night stage. "When one's employer is carted off by the minions of the law, one is not required to return any fees. If you'll consult a volume of Blackstone, Harry, you'll learn that that is a well-established point of British law."

"No doubt."

Jennie, who'd been perched on a wardrobe trunk in the wings, came walking across to them. "As I recall, Harry, you invited me to dinner." She tapped the small watch pinned to the bosom of her checkered traveling suit.

Lorenzo rubbed at his ample side whiskers with a gloved hand. "My fault entirely, my dear," he apologized. "I've dawdled here far too long investigating the possibilities of this change of venue for my justly revered evening of amazing illusions and overwhelming feats of magic. You two go along to dinner."

"I promised Roger Barksdale that I'd keep his identity secret," said the pretty reporter. "So my series of stories for the *New York Inquirer* will be somewhat vague on details. Still, I'm curious to know how you and the Wonder located us this evening."

Harry put an arm around her slim waist. "No doubt Lorenzo had another of his visions."

"Exactly, dear Jennie." The magician plucked a bouquet of a half dozen yellow roses out of the air, bowed, handed them to her. "Through a series of clever deductions, I surmised that young Barksdale was indeed the Somerset Wonder." He straightened up, reached a chocolate éclair out of the air.

"And?" she inquired, holding the bouquet close to her face.

"I decided to call on him at the cozy cottage he resides in on the Barksdale estate," Lorenzo continued. "Before I had a chance to do little more than tell him I knew his secret, I was visited with a particularly vivid vision. I saw you, Harry, and a fellow I assumed was the missing Dr. Donne imprisoned in a gloomy vault. You were tied up there in the midst of corpses, as well being threatened by Lily Hope and Sir Danvers, who looked especially menacing. As soon as I outlined my vision to young Barksdale, he exclaimed, "By Jove, old man, I've been an absolute Charlie. Gad, sir, my very own father is involved and yet I never suspected him. He's in cahoots with that notorious spy and he's kidnapped not only my mentor but your two American friends. That vault you described must be the old Barksdale Family tomb. You're a very gifted man, not only perhaps the world's greatest illusionist but also possessed of very impressive psychic—"

"My curiosity is satisfied," cut in Jennie.

"He had a few more things to say about my abilities before he admitted he was the Somerset Wonder and invited me to accompany him on his rescue mission. If you'd care to—"

"I won't be able to use most of what you've already told me in my stories. So there's no need for more."

"We'll dine now," said Harry as he took hold of the young woman's hand. "Thanks for getting us rescued, Lorenzo. And I've always been fond of your green smoke." He guided Jennie toward the wings.

"You can mention in one of your articles, without betraying any secrets," called the magician, "that the Great Lorenzo, who'll be touring the Eastern United States next month with his fabled evening of world-famous tricks, illusions, and mysteries, had a hand in the apprehension of a gang of international spies."

Jennie stopped, looked back, smiling. "You really ought to emulate the Somerset Wonder and do your good deeds anonymously."

"Anonymity," said the Great Lorenzo, "does not appeal to me."

✗

THE HOUNDS OF BASKETBALLVILLE

By Hal Charles

I

Kelly Locke brushed her Katie Couric-styled auburn hair out of her eyes and glanced down at her iPhone again. Matthew Locke was usually late for their infrequent breakfasts, but this time he was very late. As they had checked in to his hometown Basketville Inn around midnight the night before, she told herself that her Chief of Detectives father was probably just tired out from yesterday's all-day meeting with the mayor back in the city where they worked, the two-legged flight to Lexington, and the rental-car drive into the mountains. Inhaling the country air tinged with the smell of grits and bacon, Kelly was happy she had accompanied her dad, a center on the state championship basketball team that was being recognized that night in a 50th-Anniversary celebration. Across the dining room, four loud-talking people sitting around a hand-carved table vied for attention with her cell, so while she was waiting, she was trying to figure why the three shaggy-haired men and tall, flannel-shirted woman looked familiar.

Like the news reporter she was, she had just caught a snippet of their conversation—"obviously what we thought it was"—when she felt a hand on her shoulder.

"Sorry I'm late, honey," apologized the raspy voice of her father, "but I just got off the phone." He sat down, putting a calico napkin in his lap. "Persuaded my old buddy Bev Dezarn to join us for breakfast. He was the 1-guard on the team—that was before people started calling them point guards—and now he's sheriff of Clement County."

They had just started on their biscuits, gravy, and home fries when Kelly spotted a uniformed officer enter the Inn's dining room. Her highly opinionated, not-too-subtle co-anchor on Channel 4's *The Six O'Clock Report*, Chuck Mann, would have stereotyped the lawman as "Barney Fife escaped from the old-folks home."

"'Walking Stick,'" the approaching man almost shouted, giving her rising father a bear hug.

"'Walking Stick'?" Kelly questioned, her eyes absorbing her father's six-two, 240-pound frame.

"I might have been a tad thinner back when I played for the Greyhounds," Matthew Locke admitted, his mid-western accent seeming to magically transform into an Appalachian drawl. Then he introduced Kelly to his old friend.

"You're the spitting image of your maw," said Sheriff Dezarn. "We all hated to hear she had passed, which is one reason I'm sure your dad didn't want to come back too often to where he met her. Too many of those Bob Hope 'thanks for the memories.'"

Sheriff Dezarn had just started his second cup of the strongest coffee Kelly'd ever tasted when he broke from the nostalgic conversation they'd been having about who was still doing what to whom to nod at the quartet Kelly had observed earlier. "Those four gonna cause a passel of trouble before they leave."

Looking at their flannel shirts that seemed a little too warm for the first days of fall and the carefully styled unkempt hair, Kelly asserted, "They're not from around here, are they?"

"Long way between Clement County and Fantasy Land," commented the Sheriff.

"Of course," said Kelly, realizing suddenly why they looked familiar. "They're from that reality TV series *Monster Trackers*. They go all over the country trying to find the hogzillas and crocks in the sewers. What could they be doing in eastern Kentucky?"

"Got an email from their producers saying they was coming," said the Sheriff. "Claimed they had absolute proof that the lair of the Appalachian Ape was out there in the Daniel Boone National Forest."

With that, Sheriff Dezarn and her father began to laugh. It started like a few drops of rain, but then became a loud thunderstorm.

"Am I missing something?" asked Kelly, nearly drowning in the raucous laughter.

"The Appalachian Ape's a local ritual round here," said her father between guffaws. "Mostly kids, of course."

"Once a year about the time school is starting up," chimed in the Sheriff, "local boys—usually the football team—go out in the Forest and pull a few pranks. They'll leave some fur on the trees, make loud noises up on Banshee Ridge, and set some large tracks down by the Kentucky River. Even got old man Perkins's goat one year … I mean, killed it dead."

"Nobody knows how the pranks all started," said Matthew Locke, "but the kids like to terrorize the tourists and hikers by making them think we got our own version of one of the Himalayan abominable snowmen roaming these hills."

"And now those fools from Hollywood have fallen for it," said the Sheriff.

"Ah," said Kelly, "the game's a big-foot."

"You'll have to excuse her, Bev," said Kelly's now-chuckling father, "but I guess when you've read every one of Sherlock's adventures a dozen times, you can't resist a little Holmesian humor."

Just then Sheriff Dezarn's cellphone rang. He answered and just listened. Then he hung up. "Come on with me," he said, his tone suddenly serious. "Might have to call off tonight's celebration. Our starting five is down to four. They just found Billie Reynolds in the Daniel Boone National Forest looking like he'd been mauled by a bear."

II

By the time Sheriff Dezarn's patrol car reached the National Forest, the Kentucky State Police had already yellow-taped an area that was in danger of being trampled by a mob. A lone trooper was trying to prevent the scene from being contaminated.

"Since social networking replaced scanners," commented Matthew Locke, "crime scenes seem to draw twice as many people twice as fast."

"Amen, Walking Stick," said Dezarn. "Looks like a parolee's convention out here."

"Sorry, Sheriff," said one of the onlookers, a tall man in a Woodhole Wackers T-shirt; "but since you was the last to run me and my brother in, this time we showed love for the flat-hats and gave them the call."

"KSP," translated Dezarn. "This here is Houston, oldest of the Bowser brothers. He has become a real connoisseur of license plate-making, while his brother, Bennie Lee, over there is a some-time associate at our local Walmart."

"Found the body, we did surely," said Bennie Lee, pulling a cigarette wrapping paper out of his t-shirt pocket.

"Good work, Yoda," said the Sheriff. "I suppose you two weren't up here cutting your left-handed tobacco?"

"Didn't I read that marijuana is now Kentucky's number one cash crop?" said Kelly.

"That's only because no one's created a meth plant yet," said Dezarn.

"We'd have the vic covered by now," said Kelly's father to no-body in particular.

"People round here don't say 'vic,'" commented Sheriff Dezarn as he stooped down over the body. "Crime's more personal than in the big city. That's Billie … or was."

Kelly noticed that a black van had just pulled up and the four Monster Trackers were striding toward them followed by a film crew.

"Obviously the victim got too close to its lair," said the flannel-shirted woman. As though it were nothing more than a limbo bar, she lifted up the yellow tape so the others could pass under it.

"You're right, Doc," said a ducking, shaggy-haired male with a German accent. "Check out the facial marks."

"Heinrich's right." Another male knelt down over the body. "The blow, the claw marks obviously came from above."

"Obviously quite consistent with being struck by a seven-foot-tall creature," said another male, turning an unlit cigar between his lips.

"Excuse me, Mr. Celebrity," said Sheriff Dezarn, grabbing the kneeling man by his flannel collar and yanking him up. "You may know your exotic bigfoot species and all, but I'm surprised you don't recognize your basic All-American crime scene. And in case you're one of the vision-challenged, allow me to read those strange marks on the yellow tape we call words—DO NOT CROSS." With that, he ushered them all back under the tape.

"And I'm surprised you don't know me," called the woman defiantly. "I am Dr. Zara Seigler, the eminent cryptozoologist, and my team," she announced, gesturing for a camera and sound man, "are the famed Monster Trackers."

"And I am the eminent Beverly Dezarn, Sheriff of Clement County, who, if you find your way into my crime scene again, will put your butts in the local pokey for the entirety of your next cable season."

As the four retreated toward a grove of locust trees, Kelly, who had also crossed into the crime scene, was starting to backpedal when she noticed something. "Sheriff, your victim has his right hand clenched into a fist. Rigor?"

"Won't know till the doc sticks a thermometer up his … let me take a look-see." Dezarn bent down and slowly unclenched the victim's hand. In it was what looked to Kelly like two Mexican pesos.

Dezarn and Matthew Locke looked at each other in obvious shock. Finally, Kelly's father blurted out, "How can that be?"

III

Kelly and her father were sitting at a wrought-iron table in front of the Sheriff's office. Dezarn came outside with an old record player and a 33 and a 1/3 record. "Don't know if this relic'll still play, but let's give it a whirl."

He plugged it in, set the needle in the groove, and a familiar theme from Kelly's childhood began to play. Her dad had loved the old song, but she had never known why.

"*The Magnificent Seven*," she recognized.

"Great song," said her father, "till they started using it for those Marlboro commercials."

"Still," said Dezarn, "it'll always be our song."

"Who's the 'we'?" probed Kelly. Her dad had always been the strong, silent, John Wayne type who never liked to talk about himself.

"The Magnificent Seven," said Matthew Locke. "Not those cowboys, but us."

Dezarn sat down, put his cowboy-booted feet on the table, and began to hum along with the Elmer Bernstein song. "Me and Walking Stick and the other guys knew we had something special back before our championship year. I remember it like yesterday … 1960, our sophomore year, Billie 'BB' Reynolds, Rosey

Rosenberg, "Pistol" Pete Remaley, Jack "B. Quick" Culross, and Dell "Boom Boom" Cannon, we all went up to Lexington to see that movie. Only it wasn't a Mexican town we were gonna save—it was our own Basketville."

"And by beating that Louisville team in the state finals in '62," said Matthew Locke, "we did."

"Excuse me," interrupted a voice, "I couldn't help but overhear, and I'd like to listen to this discussion."

Kelly looked up to see a man in his forties who was wearing a black leather jacket and carrying a digital recorder. His face was extremely thin with a Kirk Douglas-like cleft in his chin.

"My name's Carl Michaels. I live up in Crestview and do feature work for newspapers in the Cincinnati and Louisville areas. I came out here to research a piece on the greatest upset in the history of the Commonwealth's Sweet 16 Tournament, or the greatest choke, depending on your point of view, and I think I got more than I bargained for."

"Have a seat, Mr. Michaels," said the Sheriff. "You came to the right place."

"Just under bad circumstances," added Matthew Locke.

"I know. I was just up at the forest interviewing some witnesses."

"Bowser boys ain't never witnessed anything but a lot of their own stupidity," said the Sheriff. "I'm surprised they even found Billie's body. Course I suspect they were getting ready to harvest their marijuana crop, and poor Billie, who, if my contacts are right, was probably helping them."

"So now you've got a glut of stories," said Kelly, her own reportorial senses cutting in. "A basketball reunion, a gruesome death, and a possible bigfoot event."

"Bigfoot?" said the reporter incredulously.

Sheriff Dezarn started snickering. "You never heard the local legends then?"

"I didn't put much stock in them," said Michaels.

"And now?" said Kelly.

"I'm open to all possibilities," said the reporter, "but can we get back to what you were discussing when I … intruded?"

"Hard to believe we all lasted for fifty years after that game," said Dezarn, "and Billie dies before we can get together one more time."

"Might just be karma," commented the reporter, "and karma is a bitch."

IV

When Kelly strolled down Main Street to the McCord and Schwitters Funeral Home, she found the Monster Trackers already filming at the front door. She couldn't help but notice her father's reaction to the Mexican pesos in Billie Reynolds's hand and wanted to ask him about it, but with the reporter there, the time wasn't right.

"So, Mr. McCord, you are both the county coroner and run your own mortuary," Dr. Seigler was saying in an accusatory tone.

"No conflict of interest there," chimed in the man with the German accent.

Kelly observed Mr. McCord, a white-haired man who looked so uncomfortable. Poor guy, thought Kelly. The worst he's ever dealt with before is a grieving family.

McCord said, "I've had the body less than an hour—"

"But your curiosity got the better of you," said Dr. Seigler, sounding like a courtoom prosecutor, "and you're already done an examination."

"Yes."

The sound and camera men moved in closer. Noonday sweat began to run down McCord's neck.

"And having studied the wounds," said Dr. Seigler, "you are ready to pronounce judgment."

"You mean about the cause of death," stammered McCord. "It's too early to—"

"Choose your words carefully, sir," advised Heinrich. "We have a permanent record."

"Just say it," urged Dr. Seigler. "The victim was mauled by an Appalachsquatch."

"A what?" said McCord.

"How can you deny the marks are consistent with the familiar strike response of an interrupted Appalachsquatch?" chimed in another of the Trackers.

"Excuse me, Mr. McCord," Kelly interrupted, "but I really need to talk to you about arrangements—"

"We're done here," announced Dr. Seigler. "John,' she said, turning to the cameraman, "you'd better get me some B-roll here. I can already tell this episode's going to need a lot of filler."

When the Monster Trackers had disappeared, McCord said, "I thank you. As I don't know you, I'm sure you were just being nice and ridding me of those self-important, would-be scientists."

Kelly introduced herself.

"Ah, Matt's daughter. He and I went to school together," said McCord, relaxing a bit.

"I know you haven't had much time to study the wounds," said Kelly, "but what's your best guess?"

McCord stared deeply into her eyes. "I can see you're serious, so I'll tell you the truth. The closest thing I've ever seen to this was when Mabel Jo MacEnroe got attacked by a bear that found her in his blackberry patch." He paused. "But what killed Billie? I don't know. I just don't know."

V

Kelly met her father for lunch at what he called his favorite spot, the Rocking Robin Café. The décor was very retro, the walls decorated with a mixture of 45 records and pictures of cars with fins.

"I'm sorry this weekend isn't working out the way it should have," said Kelly.

"Focus on the good," said her father. "You and I got to travel together, and without this event I doubt I would ever have brought you back to the old hometown."

"Do the good memories outweigh the bad?" asked Kelly.

He smiled across the red plastic table. "Your mother and I used to come here once a week, and if Sammy hadn't replaced the tables, you probably could have found our initials carved in one of them."

As the Cokes, fries, and burgers arrived, Kelly said, "I saw something on your face when you saw those pesos in Billie Reynolds' hand."

Matthew Locke pulled his wallet from his pocket. Opening it, he removed a Mexican peso that looked like the ones she had seen earlier in the day.

"Ah," said Kelly, "I'm sure there's a story here."

Matthew Locke put down his cheeseburger. "Right after we saw that movie—remember we were kids then—we thought we needed something real, something tangible rather than just the name *The Magnificent Seven*, so we went to a coin shop and got seven pesos. Then back in shop class we stamped the number 7 on each of them." He looked away for a moment. "This morning when I saw those pesos in Billie's fist … I could just make out … a large 7 on each of them, but what was Billie doing with two?"

VI

At six o'clock on the dot, Sheriff Dezarn picked up Kelly and a much more upbeat father at the Inn in what he called his "Lawman's Limo." As soon as they got in the back seat, he said, "I've got a few things for you. Check out that newspaper."

Kelly flipped on an overhead light and picked up a copy of *The Woodhole Gazette* dated three weeks earlier. On page one a story entitled "A Yeti Yet Again?" leapt out at her. She skimmed through it. Apparently a couple of hikers on the Appalachian Trail reported seeing a huge, hairy, ape-like creature bulling its way through the woods.

She handed the paper to her father. "Interesting. You think that somebody on the West Coast saw this information, Sheriff, and sent in the creepy quartet?"

"Who ya gonna call?" Dezarn laughed. "Got me the same idea. No matter what people think, Basketville ain't Mayberry. I know a lotta folks—mostly drug dealers—use Google to troll the Internet for things they need, so I called me a friend out in West Hollywood I met at one of those sheriff conventions and asked him what he knew about the Monster Trackers. He told me that according to *Variety* that show was on the verge of cancellation unless they drew big ratings this year. Then I checked Google myself about recent monster sightings. Discounting some giant carp in the Mississippi and a huge hog in Arkansas, I'd say Basketville's Appalachian Ape is their best chance at a big score."

"Hmm," said Kelly, "I wonder how far they'd go for a headline-grabbing bigfoot episode."

"Like staging a sasquatch killing," said Matthew Locke. "Sounds like a plot right out of Hollywood."

"We're here," announced Dezarn.

They arrived at Basketville High School with the siren blaring and the lights flashing. Everybody had agreed that the celebration should go on since "Billie would have wanted it that way." As they stepped out, they were greeted by another surprise.

"Didn't want to spoil it for you," said Dezarn, pointing to the banner above the gymnasium door. "Mayor Whitlock and the town council met last week and voted on this occasion to honor the Greyhounds by permanently changing the town's name. As the sign says, WELCOME TO BASKETBALLVILLE."

Exiting their "limo," Kelly noticed the Monster Tracker's black van pulled up to the side of the high school. As they walked in, Dezarn glad-handed so many citizens that Kelly realized that sheriffs were as much politicians as law enforcement officers. Two men approached them, both of whom Kelly recognized from earlier that day.

"What are you two doing here?" said Dezarn to the still t-shirt-wearing Bowser brothers.

"Don'cha recall," said Bennie Lee, "that Jack Culross is our uncle."

"In Clement County," said Houston Bowser, "the family tree is more like a family bush. 'Spect you and I are probably distant cousins?"

"I surely hope not," said Dezarn as he led Matthew and Kelly across the gym floor.

Kelly watched as her father was also overwhelmed by old friends and classmates. Many of them commented on how young her father looked. Probably widows or divorcees, Kelly decided as she started regarding all the memorabilia from the 1962 championship team. From the back of the gymnasium came "The Man Who Shot Liberty Valance." With so many trophies, pom-poms, and pictures, she could really grasp what a magic moment that victory must have been. In basketball-crazy Kentucky, underdog little mountain schools rarely triumphed over their bigger brothers in Louisville and Lexington.

A couple of pictures caught her eye. In a grainy one labeled "1960 Jayvees" she saw the entire Magnificent Seven. Small schools back then, her father had told her years ago, played the whole game with no more than six or seven kids on the team. The largest photograph showed the winning team hoisting the championship trophy, but something was odd about it. She counted the players. Six. Why only six? Had one of them gotten injured?

"Hey, girl," came the interruption, "you want to get out on the dance floor and do the peppermint twist with your old man?"

"Sure, Dad … if you'll explain this picture to me. Why are there six players in the championship picture and seven in the jayvee? Weren't you the Magnificent Seven?"

Matthew Locke stared past the trophy case picture. "In all the hubbub I almost forgot about that. You see, right after Christmas break our senior year Coach Ferguson called an emergency team meeting to tell us he had to kick Dell 'Boom Boom' Cannon off the team. Cops spotted him driving off from the scene from a gas station robbery. Dell and his family lived up in Birch Hollow and didn't have much money or anything."

"Seems pretty circumstantial," said Kelly as they headed onto the dance floor.

"Except one of our players saw him coming out of the gas station with a gun. Billie had no choice but to tell the police what he knew. Now let's go round and round, up and down."

Kelly had to admit her father could still twist her in knots, but when the song ended, she said, "Whatever happened to 'Boom Boom'?"

"Sad story. Looking for a job with the family disgraced here, his father moved them to Cincinnati. An old classmate called me a few years back and said he'd heard that Dell put a gun to his head and ended it."

Sheriff Dezarn cut in on them.

"Do you want to dance, too?" Kelly said.

"Rain check," said Dezarn. "Wish I had time. Got me some problems."

Matthew Locke said, "Don't tell me some of the boys are pouring homemade brew into the punch bowl?"

"That I could handle," admitted Dezarn.

"The Monster Trackers actually found the Appalachsquatch," tried Kelly.

"No, Rosey and Pistol Pete are here," said the Sheriff, "but no sign of the Bowser boys's Uncle Jack."

"That doesn't surprise me," said Kelly's father. "He came back from Nam with his body intact but a lot of his mind missing. I always held out hope the VA could truly help him."

"I've asked Mayor Whitlock to delay the ceremony until we can go fetch him from his cabin down by the Kentucky River," said the Sheriff. "Just wouldn't be right without him … and Billie."

"Mind if I tag along in the Limo?" asked Kelly.

"Breaking Up Is Hard to Do" was trying to lure them back onto the dance floor, but Kelly's mind had focused on a phrase from the Sherlock Holmes story "Silver Blaze," "the dog that didn't bark."

Someone else she had expected to see that night hadn't shown.

VII

As the squad car snaked its way down toward the Kentucky River, Matthew Locke glanced over his shoulder to see a parade of headlights trailing them. "Breaker, 10-4, looks like we got us a convoy."

Kelly pulled out her iPhone, thinking of the cases The Great Detective could have solved if he'd had one. "How long ago did Dell Cannon die?"

"Three years this month," said Sheriff Dezarn, whom Kelly was beginning to realize was certainly no Barney Fife.

"You'll get great service on that thing," promised Dezarn. "Last year Mayor Whitlock got a federal grant. The Mountain Communications Initiative upgraded everyone's service."

Dezarn was right. All five bars sloped up. Very quickly she had Cannon's obituary from the *Cincinnati Enquirer*. According to it, he passed away in Crestview, leaving behind a wife and one child, a son, Carl. Cannon would have been about her father's age, but the accompanying photo was him in his 40s. She held up the iPhone.

"When I saw that JV picture at the high school, I began to wonder, and then when I didn't see a certain someone at the celebration, my Holmes instincts kicked in. Who have we seen recently who's the spitting image of 'Boom Boom' Cannon—and from Crestview?"

"That's Culross's cabin right there," interrupted Dezarn, "and that ain't his car in front."

"My God," exclaimed Matthew Locke. "Why didn't I see this before?"

"I'm pretty sure, Dad, that reporter, Carl Michaels, is actually Dell's son."

VIII

Hearing noise and seeing the door ajar, Dezarn shouldered his way inside, his hand on his .38. Kelly and her father followed closely. Behind them, the caravan from town slid into the loose dirt on the banks of the Kentucky River.

"Your deduction was right, Kelly," said Matthew Locke, quickly showing the Sheriff the picture on Kelly's iPhone.

"Carl Michaels is Dell's son?" Sheriff Dezarn shook his head.

"Our supposed reporter has the same Kirk Douglas chin as your former teammate," said Kelly. Then, catching the tableau in front of her, she stepped back.

Carl Michaels stood behind the slightly balding man sitting in an overstuffed chair. Michaels had one arm around the neck of his victim. In his other hand he held a baseball bat that had been pierced with several large nails.

"I guess your father told you all about the Appalachian Ape," said Dezarn.

"That's not all he told me," said Michaels. "You stay back or I'll really smack him."

Just then the momentary silence was broken by a shriek from the open doorway. "Lord," said a red-faced Bennie Lee Bowser, "don't whack Uncle Jack!"

Dezarn body-checked a rushing Houston Bowser, then raised his .38 and said under his breath, "I'm afraid I'll hit Jack."

To distract Michaels, Kelly took a step to the left of the Sheriff. "All this for revenge."

"As Dad used to say," snarled Michaels, "'You betchum, Red Ryder.'"

Kelly continued, "And you started with Billie Reynolds because you think he stole your dad's position on the basketball team."

"Think. I don't think, I know. He's the one who was the only eyewitness to that gas station robbery. Dad always said Reynolds probably did it himself, then blamed Dad so he could be a starter."

"The gas station owner himself ID-ed your father, son," said Dezarn.

"Too bad Coach Ferguson went to that big arena in the sky," said Kelly's father. "He could tell you how it all played out."

"Dad thought you guys planned the whole thing just to get rid of him because he was the best. He showed me those clippings first of the seven of you, then the six. Isn't it funny you guys never mentioned him after he was kicked off the team. And what about those damned pesos—you guys were supposed to have each others's backs."

"Your dad left town. That was part of the deal his father made with Judge Spain after giving back the stolen money," said Dezarn. "Dell had to leave this community for good."

"Did you decide to kill off the remaining team members when you heard about the 50th-Anniversary celebration?" said Kelly, taking another step to her left.

"Dad must have said a million times to me, 'Carl Michael, in Kentucky basketball players are royalty, And state champs are kings for life. This guy I'm about to kill went to West Point. Dezarn became Sheriff for life. Your father is a big city policeman. The other two are successful out-of-state businessmen. Even Reynolds was a drug lord.'"

"A drug lord is a success?" said Matthew Locke.

"He seemed to think so when he agreed to meet me to sell some of his merchandise," said Carl Michael Cannon. "You should have seen his face when I paid him with Dad's peso. Now, Sheriff, put your gun down and step back."

"The two pesos in Billie's hand ... I should have realized he was trying to give us a clue to his killer since each of us had only one," said Matthew Locke under his breath.

Kelly caught her father's eye and directed his vision to the basketball sitting in a trophy stand beside him. "And what do you plan to do about all these witnesses, including that TV crew that just came through the door behind me?"

As though they had practiced it a thousand times, and in a way they had, as Dezarn placed his gun on a card table, Matthew Locke grabbed the trophy basketball and threw an outlet pass his idol, Wes Unseld, would have been proud of.

The ball struck Michaels in the nose, causing him to drop the bat. Dezarn was on top of him with a speed that belied his age, wrestling the younger man to the floor and cuffing him.

"I hope you flannel-shirted clowns have all that on tape," shouted Dr. Seigler, who had undergone a complete transformation into business suit and heels. "*Monster Trackers* may not be around to use it, but we've got enough for the pilot episode of a new reality show, *Extreme High School Reunions*."

As the relieved group walked out of the cabin ready to celebrate the anniversary, Kelly turned to her father. "Stolen legacies, hidden identities, and seemingly supernatural beasts … maybe we should call this 'The Case of the Hounds of Basketballville,' "

Her dad started to laugh when at that moment a loud roar sounding like a cross between a wounded coyote and an angry bear echoed down the hollow to the river.

The Monster Trackers, Sheriff Dezarn, Matthew Locke, and Kelly all screamed at once: "The Appalachsquatch!"

HIT ONE OUT OF THE PARK

by Jeff Baker

You're supposed to look after your little brother. Keep him out of trouble. At least that's how it's supposed to work. But that's how I got involved with a gambling ring, a murder plot and Joe DiMaggio's baseball bat. The one we accidentally sort of stole.

The main reason for all of this was a guy named Diedrich. He ran a respectable grocery store in our New York neighborhood, with a few sidelines. Mainly playing the horses, betting on ballgames and the like. All of it under the table, or rather out of the back of his store. And my brother Ward Keaton was a regular customer, making a nice pile off of a lot of betting which our Mother would not have approved and which I barely approved. Things went really bad in June of 1941. Diedrich managed to stiff my brother out of $200, which he said he'd placed on a game like Ward had asked him to. Then Diedrich says he never made the bet. Swore it up and down. My brother did a lot of swearing, too. Then he did some threatening. As a consequence he was officially thrown out of Diedrich's store, front and back rooms.

Me, I heard the whole thing when I got off work. Yeah, I worked on a loading dock but looking after Ward was a full-time job, too.

"George," Ward said, "two-hundred bucks is no ten grand but it is a lot of money. And it isn't his."

I tried to get him to calm down but that wouldn't work with Ward any more than appealing to his common sense would. With my tongue planted firmly in my cheek and trying not to mumble I suggested calling the police. That just made him madder. He started talking about "going down to Diedrich's and pulling my money outa him with a crowbar."

Fortunately he wouldn't go down there alone and he couldn't get me to go along. I managed to talk him into sleeping on it.

Unfortunately, he slept on it.

The next morning he'd dreamed up an idea: do away with Diedrich and get his money and maybe more besides. I remembered

Ward almost getting us in trouble for shoplifting when we were kids. And he'd started more than his share of fights. But neither of us were big guys and he'd lost a lot of the fights, including the one or two he'd dragged me into.

"Ever watch the movies?" I asked. "Ever listen to the radio? The killers never get away with it. The cops are always a couple of jumps ahead of them."

Ward agreed that he didn't know just then how he could work his way around it and I suggested that he drop the whole thing as a bad idea. And that was what I thought he did. I was breathing sighs of relief until just after the first of July when the weather was getting really hot and I was hoping that if we got into this war in Europe they'd draft me and send me to the North Pole or something. Ward showed up with a big grin on his face and a crazy look in his eye and invited me into his bedroom, which was really part of the living room with a makeshift curtain and a view of the fire escape.

"Whaddya think this is?" Ward said proudly, pulling a wrapped up something in a newspaper from under his bed.

"I dunno. What?" I said, weighing the thing in my hands.

"The perfect murder weapon," he said smiling broadly. He patted the wrapping. "Perfect because this thing can't be traced back to me and the guy I grabbed it from wasn't supposed to have it in the first place."

My mouth was hanging open. I felt like asking about a zillion questions but nothing came out. Ward nodded and his expression got serious.

"I did some thinking and I remembered Romano saying in a loose moment that he was about to come into some stuff that nobody was supposed to know about and did I want in on it? I said no but I checked it out, anyway. Pile of stuff in the back of his workshop that all looked kinda dangerous, so I went back later and took this thing. It's a good thing he usually does the stealing because it was the easiest thing in the world to take this outa there."

All of a sudden I didn't want anything to do with the whatever-it-was in my hands that was wrapped in the newspaper. I was worried that it was going to go off or something and I was relieved when Ward picked it out of my hands and tossed it on the bed.

"You haven't," I started to say. "I mean, Diedrich. Is he, you know, dead?"

Ward laughed and shook his head no.

"I've got it all planned out, see," he said. "Friday's the Fourth of July, right? Diedrich always shoots off firecrackers and gets really drunk, right?"

I nodded. Every July Fourth since repeal of Prohibition.

"So when he's loaded to the muzzle and staggering around back of his store, I sneak out of the dark and get him with this."

With that, Ward pulled the wrapping off the thing he'd put on the bed and held it in front of me. It was, yeah, a baseball bat. Wood, kinda worn in places, and the handle where someone would grab it looked really worn like someone had filed or sanded it down. I fingered the bat gingerly and felt around until I found what I was looking for, the name engraved on the bat: Joe DiMaggio.

"Don't you read the papers instead of wrapping stuff in them?" I asked. "This is the bat! His bat! It was stolen last weekend from Griffith Stadium! It's been in all the papers! On the radio! Romano pinched it and then you pinched it from him!"

"No, some guy Romano knows pinched it and then I ..." Ward began.

"No!" I said, trying to yell and keep my voice down at the same time. "You aren't going to get away with this! I'm amazed you got away with anything."

I grabbed the bat and sat down on the bed. Hard. Needless to say keeping tabs on Ward while he was planning doing someone in with a murder weapon half of New York was already looking for was making my own day the kind Mrs. Roosevelt usually didn't write about.

"Can I have my bat back?" Ward asked.

"Yeah," I said and handed it to him. Then I grabbed it back. "No! You can't have it back! It isn't even your bat! This is DiMaggio's!"

"Well, so?" Ward said.

"So," I said, thinking quickly. "What're all the kids gonna say if they find out somebody offed somebody else with DiMaggio's bat?"

Ward just stared and blinked a couple of times.

"And what about DiMaggio?" I said. "You know how superstitious ballplayers are! This could put him in a slump, end his streak, ruin his career maybe."

"You think maybe?" Ward asked.

"Yeah," I said, faking all the confidence I could. "I think so. It's our responsibility to baseball not to let anything happen to that bat. Like murder."

"Yeah, well all I'm gonna do is ruin Diedrich's career," Ward said. "He didn't think about mine. And that bat's mine right now."

"Yours?"

"Yeah. I stole it. Totally honestly. Now hand it over."

"Okay," I said, handing him the bat. "But you aren't going to go any place with it right now? Flash it around the neighborhood?"

"Nahh," he said. "Not until this weekend."

I sighed. That gave me a couple more days to think. I thought about pulling something to eat out of the icebox, all the talk about DiMaggio had gotten me to thinking about ballpark hotdogs. I was sitting at the dining room table which was the table shoved up beside the icebox and the stove, about to start in on a leftover chicken leg when I heard a sudden whumping sound over and over. I rushed over to Ward's bedroom. He'd put two pillows on the bed, one on top of the other and was hitting them with the bat.

"What do you think?" he asked. "From the top or the side?"

"That's my pillow!" I said.

"Yeah, sorry." Ward said. "It's nothing personal." He started hitting the pillows again. "Probably from the back. I'll have to sneak up on him."

"What are you doing?" I asked. I knew exactly what he was doing but it was the only thing I could think of to say at the moment.

"Batting practice," he said. "I figure I'm not going to get three strikes to hit Diedrich, so I'd better make it good." He swung the bat again; really hard this time and the top pillow sailed off against the wall. I stared, wondering to myself if he'd be satisfied with just fouling Diedrich instead of permanently hitting him out.

I went back to my chicken leg. I just sat and stared at it trying not to think about how much it resembled a baseball bat.

That evening I was taking a nap when there was a banging on the apartment door. For a moment I thought Ward was practicing with the bat again but I remembered that he'd stepped out and left the bat wrapped under the bed. Then the banging came again and I was wide awake.

The guy at the door wasn't too big but he was big enough. He gave me the once over and asked to see Ward. Actually he had I-wanna-break-Ward-Keaton-in-half written all over him.

"I'm Ward's brother George. His big brother." I tried to stand up a little taller. "Ward doesn't live here any more. Hasn't for a while. May I mean, who's asking?"

I'd almost said 'May I say who's calling?' in the same super-polite tone my Grandmother always used.

"Name's Malone. Call me Malone," the big man said.

"Something else I can help you with Mister Malone?" I asked making sure I was blocking the doorway.

"Yeah," he said. "When your brother comes back here—"

"When I see him, you mean," I said.

"When you see him you tell him that Mr. Romano did an inventory and he needs to talk to him." Malone was glaring. "He'll know where to call."

With that, Malone turned around and stalked down the hallway. I closed the door as soon as he was out of sight and about collapsed. I wondered if I should've just given him the bat back. It wasn't five minutes later that Ward all but ran into the apartment looking like he was out of breath. He held up a copy of the evening paper.

Right there on the front page was a big picture of DiMaggio grinning and posed like he's about to swing the bat right into the camera. I looked closer. Yeah, it was definitely the bat we had all right.

"Look at this," Ward said. "These pictures are all over the city. All over the East Coast. The whole country is after us!" His voice had risen to a squeak. "Ted Williams is probably after us!"

And they aren't the only ones, I thought.

"This," I said, "would be a great time to lay low. To stay out of sight."

"Yeah," Ward said.

"And to not do anything that would attract, you know, undue attention," I said. I was faking it but Ward was buying it.

"Yeah, we lay low until Friday night when we knock off Died-rich during the fireworks!"

So much for that.

"We do it during the fireworks instead of after so Diedrich won't hear himself getting killed." Ward said.

I felt like hiding under my bed or just getting in bed and pulling the covers up over me until July fifth. Which made a lot less sense in the middle of summer.

"We gotta hide out somewhere," Ward said.

"Like where?" I said. "The movies?"

"Or the pool hall."

"We can't afford to sit in the movies for two or three days," I said.

"No, just until we get Diedrich."

"And we're not gonna get Diedrich," I said.

"Not right now, anyway," Ward said. He rushed over to his bed and pulled his jacket out from under it. "I've got a couple of bucks, we're hiding out at the movies."

"You're hanging out at the movies," I said.

"You wanna stay here and answer the door when that big bruiser comes back?"

I just stood there and stared. That was the first thing he'd said that made any actual sense. Ward had taken his jacket and was stuffing the bat up one sleeve.

"You're not going to wear that like that?" I said.

Ward stopped trying to hide the bat in the jacket and stared at it. If there's one thing more conspicuous than wearing a jacket like that in the heat of summer it's probably trying to sneak a baseball bat under the jacket into a theater.

Ward stared around the room. His face brightened when he saw the stove.

"Oh that's just asking for trouble," I said, imagining DiMaggio's bat going up like burned meatloaf.

"Not in the stove, dummy," Ward said. He got down on his hands and knees and slid the bat along the floor past the corner leg of the stove and into a hole in the wall I'd never noticed before.

"And it just fits, too!" Ward said triumphantly.

"Where? Into the apartment next door?" I asked.

"Naaah! Into the wall. I've used it before to hide stuff."

I just hoped that mice wouldn't make off with the bat.

I couldn't enjoy the movies. The cartoon was all about mice hiding something from a cat which made me worry even more. The newsreel was worse, a lot of baseball footage. I kept imagining the announcer saying "Dateline; New York City. Two brothers,

George and Ward Keaton, who are sitting in the middle row of this theater, are believed to be the culprits involved in the theft of Joe DiMaggio's lucky baseball bat. President Roosevelt is ordering the National Guard to close in on the suspects."

I couldn't even say what the main feature was. I wasn't really paying attention. Ward, he was just munching popcorn, happy as a clam.

When the movie was over we decided not to stay for the next showing. Maybe the idea of hanging around in the movie theater was starting to feel silly.

We'd walked out of the theater and Ward was suggesting that we find a pool hall or an all-night diner to go to when someone else spoke up.

"Mr. Keaton. And Mr. Keaton. A word with you, please."

It was just like in the movies. We turned around. There was an unfamiliar man standing there and he wasn't smiling.

"Oh, hi, Mr. Romano," Ward said.

The movies don't tell how sick you feel when something like that happens.

"Let's just keep moving," I said quietly turning back around the way we were heading.

Malone was standing there, looking bigger than he had in our doorway. Ward and I looked at each other. It was either run or fight and neither would do us much good.

"Step this way if you please," Romano said, gesturing towards a narrow alley between two buildings. I walked in, followed by Malone and Romano with Ward between them. I stared down the alleyway; it ended in a tall fence.

Romano and Malone blocked our view of the exit.

"Mister Keaton, you have something that belongs to me. Something I want very badly," Romano said.

"Really?" Ward asked.

"Yes, and you're interfering with a very important business matter. A matter that has already gone very bad."

Romano smiled; it somehow made the alley seem smaller.

"The item in question is a baseball bat," Romano said.

"Yeah," Ward said hoarsely.

"We need it now," Romano said. "And at the moment we are willing to compensate you for your efforts in returning the item to us."

To his credit my brother didn't lose his composure. I would have stood there, jaw dropped, blithering like one of the Bowery Boys. Or more than likely I would have cried. But Romano wasn't talking to me and so I just stood there stunned.

"How much compensation are we talking about?" Ward asked.

"It is worth far more to us to settle this issue now." Romano said. "Quickly and quietly."

Ward just stood and glared.

"A hundred and fifty dollars," Romano said.

"Five hundred." Ward said, unflinchingly.

"Two-hundred dollars," Romano said.

"It's worth at least a grand isn't it?" Ward said. "Who you dealing with, DiMaggio?"

"Mister Keaton, consider yourself lucky that we are in this position. Two-hundred-and-fifty and this is our final offer." Romano had stopped smiling.

"Sounds good to me." Ward said. "Now, my associate and I will go and—"

Romano cut him off.

"One of you will stay here; the other will bring the required item."

Ward and I stared at each other.

"Fine," Ward said. "My brother will go get the, uh, item."

I nodded, trying to look as calm as he was. He grinned at me, but there was a look in his eyes that was saying don't be long, Big Brother.

I walked and ran back to the apartment, checking behind me constantly, convinced that I was going to get jumped or killed every step of the way or that I'd find the apartment ransacked and the bat gone. But the apartment was fine and I was able to pull the bat out of the hole in the wall with some effort and to deliver it, wrapped in Ward's jacket back to the alleyway where I'd left Romano, Malone, and Ward.

They were just standing around talking like they were waiting on a parade to start or something instead of the return of clumsily-stolen merchandise. I handed Ward the bat and he handed it over to Romano who forked over the two-hundred-and-fifty dollars. We made fifty bucks on the deal but I figured we were just lucky to get out of it with our lives.

We spent the Fourth of July sticking close to the apartment and watching the fireworks from the window, which was better than spending it with one of us trying to murder someone and the other trying to hold him back. A little while later I read in the papers that Joe DiMaggio's bat was "recovered" over in Jersey. And not a word about us, which was fine by me. Maybe it all scared Ward enough that he stayed out of trouble from then on, unless you count the War which started up for us late that year. When Ward came back from his hitch in the Navy he sure had grown up a lot. He also had a lot more money which he said came from shipboard poker games which he swore were totally legit. I didn't know how much of that I believed but he'd shown me his best poker face that night with Romano, so I knew he could bluff with the best of them.

Me, I spent the war in the Army. I even saw DiMaggio one time when we were both overseas. Of course I didn't talk to him and I certainly didn't bring up the subject of the stolen bat with him or anyone. And I've read since that they say the disappearance of DiMaggio's lucky bat during his streak in the summer of '41 might have been just a publicity gimmick.

Of course, "they" never met my Brother...

✗

Jeff Baker has worked in fast food, where he once had to dress up as a lobster; performed comedy in local clubs and driven a delivery truck carrying everything from amaretto to zucchini. He has been published in Space and Time *magazine and* Over My Dead Body. *A 1983 graduate of Newman University, he lives in Wichita, Kansas with his significant other Darryl and "way too many Hawaiian shirts." His Facebook page is at "Jeff Baker, Author."*

TRAVELING LIGHT

by John M. Floyd

Sheriff Lucy Valentine trudged up the muddy slope to find the first rays of the sun peeking over the horizon and an ancient purple gas-guzzler parked beside her patrol car. In the dim light it looked as long as a battleship. She walked to the open driver's-side window, hooked her thumbs into her gunbelt, and said, "What are you doing here, Mother?"

Frances Valentine shoved open the car door and climbed out. "Waiting for you," she said. "The story of my life."

"How'd you know I was here?"

"I heard you blow past the house. I was up already anyhow, so I hopped in the Purple Rocket and followed you."

"I didn't use the siren—you telling me you recognize the sound of my car?"

"I do when it's going a hundred miles an hour." Fran shut her door and leaned back against it.

"I was in a hurry. Anyhow, thanks for not tromping all over the crime scene."

"I would have, but these are my good shoes," Fran said. "Fill me in."

Lucy tossed her notebook and flashlight into her cruiser, sighed, and rubbed her eyes with her knuckles like a little girl. "Bad news. Dispatch got a phone call from Buddy Johnson an hour ago, saying he'd found Pete Purwell dead in a woodshed."

"Pete Purwell?"

"Buddy said he'd been lost and looking for a place to sleep, and had tripped over Pete's body. I called the rehabilitation center—Buddy's been there since last month, remember?—and sure enough, they told me he'd escaped around three a.m." She pointed toward the Purwells's house and outbuildings, at the bottom of the hill. "And sure enough, Pete's down there dead, shot twice. Nobody else at home."

Fran nodded. "That part makes sense. Pete's no-account brothers have been bragging that they spend most nights at the casino, and their dad's been in Jackson since March."

"What's he doing down there?"

"Nursing home," Fran said. "Any sign of the murder weapon?"

"No. Just the body, and drag marks. Whoever shot Pete must've done it somewhere else, then lugged him into the shed."

It was dead quiet on the hilltop. A wispy gray fog hung over the fields to the west, between here and town. A few stubborn stars still blinked overhead. Lucy could hear her stomach growling.

"Let me get this straight," Fran said. "Buddy escaped from drug rehab in the middle of the night, and then—while on the run—phoned the police to report a murder?"

Lucy shrugged. "What can I say? He was probably scared. And nobody ever accused him of being smart."

"How'd he place the call?"

"The people at the center told me he'd grabbed a cell phone off a nurse's desk just before he flew the coop. But nothing else was missing—no pills, food, money, flashlights, weapons, anything. A guard saw him running away across the front lawn, dressed only in pajamas. And running pretty fast, apparently."

Both of them stood there a minute, picturing that.

"So what do you think?" Fran asked.

"It ain't quantum physics, Mother."

"What do you mean?"

"I mean it's obvious. Buddy Johnson's the killer."

"Why?"

"Because that woodshed was pitch dark when I got here," Lucy said. "No lanterns, no lights, no windows. And remember, Buddy ID'ed the body as Pete's, not one of the other brothers, or someone else's. To know that, he had to have seen Pete's face."

"Where would he have seen it?"

"Who knows? Maybe outside in the moonlight. Maybe in the Purwells's house. Wherever they were when Buddy killed him, before the body got dragged to the woodshed."

Another silence passed. Fran was gazing off into the hazy distance. Lucy caught a sweet whiff of honeysuckle.

Behind them, in the direction of town, a motor growled and a pair of headlights emerged over the rise. "Here comes the coroner,"

Lucy said. "I gotta go. My deputies are out looking for Buddy, and—"

"What you should be looking for," Fran said, "are the two brothers. Bernard and…"

"Elwin. I know. We already left phone messages for them."

"No, I mean bring them in for questioning. They both hated Pete, you know that. He was the oldest, and their dad's favorite. I heard he was set to inherit everything—and Old Man Purwell's past ninety." Fran paused. "In case you forgot, that's called 'motive.'"

Sheriff Valentine stared at her. "Didn't you hear what I just said? Buddy Johnson did it. He must have. Somehow he found a gun—probably Pete's—and shot him with it, then dragged him into the woodshed. Otherwise, if Buddy had just stumbled across the body they way he said he had, in the shed, he would never have been able to see Pete's face, and identify him."

Fran shook her head. "You're wrong."

The county coroner had parked and was standing ten feet away, watching them. Arguments between the two Valentines were nothing new. "Morning, ladies," he said. He sounded even sleepier than Lucy felt.

She gave him a hold-on-for-a-minute finger wave and kept her eyes on Fran. "How am I wrong?"

"You're wrong because Buddy's not the killer."

"You want to explain that?"

"What I want," Fran said, "is for you to send somebody over to the casino and bring the Purwell brothers in for questioning."

"I can't."

"You have to. And you better hope they didn't get spooked and decide to drive straight to Mexico."

Lucy studied her mother's face. "You're amazing."

"In what way am I amazing?"

"You're convinced of this, aren't you."

"I know Buddy Johnson, Lucy. He's mixed up, sure, but he wouldn't kill anyone. I also know his brothers. You're looking for the wrong man." Fran folded her arms the way she always did when she'd made up her mind. "Make the call, and bring them in. You'll see."

Lucy hesitated. "Bet you a ribeye steak I'm right."

"The Longhorn," Fran said.

"You're on."

The coroner cleared his throat. "You said you had a body for me, Sheriff?"

"Yes, I did," Lucy said. "I still do." She gave Fran a final look, then stepped past her and headed down the hill. "Follow me."

Later that morning, back at the office, Sheriff Valentine found Fran in the break room, chugging coffee. She drew a deep breath, let it out, crossed the room to Fran's table, and said, "Deputy Malone just called in. He picked up Pete's brothers, like I asked him to."

Fran just watched her, waiting.

"They were in their pickup truck, outside the casino," Lucy said. "Sleeping it off."

"And?"

She hesitated a moment. "The youngest—Elwin—did a *Perry Mason* and confessed on the spot. They killed Pete and stowed him in the woodshed. He said Bernard was in on it, too."

Fran nodded. No smile, no I-told-you-so look. "Anything on Buddy?"

"He turned up at a cafe in Batesville. He'd been hitchhiking. Still in his PJs." Lucy took off her hat and sagged into a plastic chair. "How'd you know, Mother?"

"Know what?"

"Don't give me that. How did you know Buddy was innocent?"

Fran shrugged. "I guess I didn't, for sure. But I knew how he could've seen Pete's face, and identified him, in that shed."

"How? I told you, it was pitch black in there."

Fran drained her coffee cup, grimaced, and studied her daughter's face. "Haven't you ever dropped something on the ground at night and needed to find it, or had trouble getting your key into the your back door when the garage is dark?"

"I suppose."

"So how'd you finally see to do it?"

Lucy blew out a sigh. "I don't know, I guess I fumbled around until I got it done."

"What the hell are you talking about?"

"I'm talking about cell phones." Fran took hers out of her purse and held it up. "You told me Buddy stole one from the rehab center before he left."

"And?"

"And…" She flipped her phone open and showed Lucy the illuminated display. "They make good flashlights."

Sheriff Valentine blinked. She opened her mouth to say something, then closed it again. After a long moment she nodded slowly. "I guess they do, at that."

"I agree that Buddy Johnson is no genius," Fran said. "But he isn't stupid, either."

Mother and daughter sat there staring at each other. It was suddenly so quiet Lucy could hear the hum of the electric clock on the wall of the break room.

Apparently Fran heard it, too. "Come on, it's almost lunchtime," she said, and rose from the table. "You want to stop by the bank first?"

"Why?"

She grinned. "Because the Longhorn ain't cheap."

✗

"That door is where they put the batteries."

DATE NIGHT

by S. A. Stolinsky

I picked up the phone. I couldn't imagine who'd be calling at eleven o'clock at night. My sponsor from AA usually called in the morning to give me hope for the day.

"Hello?" I said, feeling queasy.

"Hey, baby," I could hear Clarence's phony tone. He always sounded like that when he wanted girls to do things for him. He was an asshole, but he was the only asshole in town right now for me. One more DUI and I was through. They'd threatened to put me in Lynwood Correctional and throw away the key. Fuck them. Fuck Clarence. I put on my navy pea coat. I knew I was going to the bar. If I didn't he'd fire my ass.

"It's a councilman," he said. "A big, fat councilman. You can show him all you got."

I thought I'd puke. I yelled into the kitchen to my mother and said I didn't know when I'd be back. I shoved my hair up into a loose pony-tail. I'd take it down at the bar.

It was a rusty night. Lots of people think I talk funny, but when I say "rusty" I mean it was windy and brisk-like. You could feel the sharp edges of the wind on your face. I love that. I closed the front door. I don't know whether my mother heard me or not and frankly I could care less. She wouldn't give a rat's ass anyway. Ever since they took my kid away. She hates me for giving up her grandchild. But I liked the couple that adopted him. They were professional, you know? People who had money. They'd do good by him, I knew that.

Outside I got in the truck. The driver's side door was stiff and creaky. Needed oil or something. If Eddie ever found out I was drivin' it at night, he woulda kicked my ass. But hell, he's in jail. He's lucky somebody's taking care of his old junk-heap anyway. And I'm still pissed at him for showing my picture to all his con friends inside. That was private. You never know who's seeing your shit all over the net now. I swear. There I am in my birthday suit and he's showin' it all over the cell block. And he's in the shadows of the picture. Probably embarrassed he's got like a two inch dick. I hate that man sometimes.

It's only like ten minutes from the trailer park to the bar. Ma and me got lucky with the trailer. It was the only one left and it was newly painted. The guy who sold it to us even left the green awning. He went to live on his son's boat or some shit, I forget.

The evening was cold, but it was clear. I turned left out of the trailer park into the main street and it was empty. I mean, empty. Not a car in sight. I went slow. You never know when some dork'll come slamming out of his driveway and t-bone you, especially if he's been drinkin'.

I drove a block to the interstate. I could see the neon flashing on and off in the distance. One of those tipsy electric cocktail glasses that flicker on and off with "Bar, Bar, Bar" under 'em. Like I say, the joint was only like ten minutes away. That wasn't the point. I was just tired. My breath smelled like the bottom of a birdcage even though I gargled with mouthwash before I left the house.

The interstate had some cars comin' in the other direction, but it sure was quiet for a Saturday night. Suburbs outside L.A., man, you'd think there'd be more action. Sometimes they're quieter than the boonies.

I turned left into the bar's parking lot. One of the red lights of the neon was out, of course. God forbid Clarence, the owner'd, spring to get it fixed. It'd probably cost him a dollar to do that. Uh uh. Not Clarence. He'd rather have the place look like the out-of-town dump it was.

I got out of the car and let my hair down. It'd grown at least four inches since I got out of rehab. Practically down to my waist. Everybody always says when you're in your early twenties your hair grows like crazy. When you hit thirty it slows down. Man I'm only twenty-four. I can't even imagine hitting thirty. I walked toward the entrance.

You should see this place. The door's got these little square-like peek-a-boo windows surrounded by wood. Like it's been hand carved, right? Probably mass produced in some half-lit garage somewhere downtown L.A. The door handle is this big old brass thing you have to take in both hands and then press a lever to make it open. It's a bar and a pool hall, for Criss' sake. Not the entrance to Graceland. The entrance is like hidden under a wood roof that kind of hangs over the front door. I guess to save people from getting wet if it rains. I pulled the door open. It was a heavy sucker.

Inside there were three or four heavies, you know the big guys, too much pumping iron at Gold's Gym, maybe 'roids, although with the guts these guys had, maybe not. I walked to the bar and lifted the rail. Philie was tending bar—servin.' Her real name is Philimina. She's from one of those islands in the Pacific. Her skin's nice, and she has huge black eyes and shoulder-length straight black hair, but I know she's not as pretty as me. That's why Clarence got me out here. I'm tellin' ya, for him—anything for a buck. Clarence was in the office, a cubicle room with no windows hidden behind dirty maroon-colored curtains on a rod.

"Hey," Philie says to me, like I'm her best friend now. "So you made it, huh?"

"I'm here," I says, "so, yeah, I guess I did."

She comes in close. I hate that, people who come up real close to you like they're gonna tell you the secret of the ages or some shit. The three assholes drinking beer from the tap look up. One of 'em gives me the smile that says my ass is tight. I think I know that, dorko.

"Hey, baby," one fat slob says. "How much?"

"Shut the fuck up." I says.

Clarence yanks the curtain aside and comes out just as this guy slips off the stool, like he's gonna come at me. I don't think so. Not with Clarence right there.

"Tell your 'hoes to watch their mouths, C," he says.

Clarence nods and then comes up to me and opens a couple of buttons on my coat so my cleavage shows good. I'm wearing what I wore to work this morning, but nothin' underneath, you know?

He says, "Hey, baby, get in something comfortable. I'm gonna introduce you to Mr. Right."

"Mr. Right? Is that his real name?"

"No, baby, but he wants anonymity." Clarence says, putting his face close to mine like we're gonna rub noses. He pushes my hair behind my ears. Then he kisses my forehead. "Big pay day tonight."

I don't know why, but I could feel myself gettin' madder and madder. I like money and when the woman who adopted my kid sends me a picture at Christmas I'd like to send a little extra cash to the kid, with a note, if she'd let me. I suddenly feel like crying. I take things real hard.

Anyway, Clarence goes in the back and I go to the ladies room and there's this off the shoulder spandex thing with sequins around a real low neckline and the same sequin pattern on the sleeveless arm-holes. It's hangin' on a rod that must have been a shower fixture at one time. The bustier is a size small and usually I take a small to medium, but I mean, this thing's small. There's no pants, so I'm assuming Clarence doesn't care what I wear on the bottom. The thing is see-through, too. Like that clear handkerchief type see-through. It looked like a rodeo skank'd wear it. It wasn't L.A.

In L.A., you'd go down to Melrose and Robertson, you know, and go into some of those shops and even if you couldn't really afford it, you'd put something sexy and nice on your credit card, cause, like those pieces are nice. I read *Elle* and they call the good stuff "pieces." I pulled off my top and laid it across the filthy sink he never has cleaned. I suppose that'll end up being one of my jobs pretty soon, too.

I put the sequin top on. It fit snugger than I thought. I mean, man, you could see everything. Clarence didn't want me wearing a bra. I'm pretty well-built. Twenty-four inch waist and a thirty-eight D cup. My hips are wide. It fit tight. I put my pea coat over it.

I went into the main bar area. The three slobs were gone from the bar and a tiny lady was sitting sipping some drink with a flower in it. I didn't even know we made those. I mean this job I got like a week ago, studied the bartending manual a couple of nights at home and never did get to the part of making a drink with some damn flower in it. Probably plastic. I could hear voices in the inner office. Clarence musta heard me come out of the bathroom.

"Get in here, sweetheart," he yelled in.

I slid back the greasy curtain separating his office from the main area. There was a pool hall on the other side of the bar, but I never think about that because I never have any reason to go back there. I just forget it. Maybe when I'm in this job longer I'll be going back there to serve drinks or something. I walked into his office. I'd been there before when he hired me, but it looked smaller at night. No window. That always makes a space look smaller.

Clarence was sittin' in a swivel chair behind a big desk which took up most of the room and had a land line phone and lots of papers and shit on it. It faced the entrance. Clarence loved to lie back in the swivel and put his feet, crossed of course, on the table top. Made him feel important, I guess. Behind him on the cork board wall were fight posters. Now, I never knew Clarence to be a fighter or a fight fan, he never mentioned anything, but like I say, I've only worked here a week. A tiny red-shaded light gave the only light in the room, a pale cherry color.

Clarence didn't look like no fighter. He was built like a fire plug. Small head, big trunk, short legs, short arms. Put on a green top and he could have gone to a Halloween party as an avocado. I had to smile when I thought of that, but I'm sure he thought I was just being sweet. He looked steady at me as I came through the curtain.

"You changed?" He said, sitting forward and putting his elbows on the table. He was smoking a cigarette and it was down to the last ash. Stank up the whole room.

I opened up the pea coat. He sat forward and laughed out loud.

"Show Mr. Willfield here, will ya, baby?"

I turned, holding my coat flaps open.

"This is Mr. Bob Willfield," he said, nodding his head to the far corner of the room where there was no light.

I looked over. I couldn't see anyone, but I could hear someone breathing real loud, like they were a smoker. I was surprised I hadn't heard it when I came in. Then as my eyes got used to the dim of the room, I made out a small fat guy in a black or grey business suit, it was hard to tell in the dark, wearing a tie on a dark shirt. He had on real shiny shoes that laced up. His hands were folded over his paunch, the fingers locked together like a guy who's resting back after eating a big meal.

I let my coat flaps close and cupped my hands over my eyes to focus.

"Hi," I said.

"Hi," Bob said back. "Call me 'Bob' honey. I like to be called Bob."

He had a deep, real melodic type voice. Like someone you hear on a radio. "You got a real nice body, honey."

"You two get going," Clarence said, like he owned me. I was startled. I looked at him and for a second I couldn't move, like when someone you kind of like shouts at you and you didn't realize they had that in them.

I turned and walked out without answering him. I just went back into the bathroom, found my skirt and put it on. I looked in the mirror. My grandma's heart necklace was around my neck. It's the only thing she left me when she died. Of alcoholism, they said, but it was because her husband ran off twenty-five years earlier. Women don't get over that easy. I was debating if I should keep it around my neck. It was kind of personal. I don't see why I should share that with this little fat Bob. I put it in my purse.

I hung my uniform up so it wouldn't wrinkle. You have to pay for your uniform yourself, but if you have no money, like, hell, I don't, Clarence takes it out of your first week's pay. Twenty-five dollars. I walked out of the bathroom. Philie was sweating over the hot water washing glasses and she didn't even look up at me when I came out. I pushed the curtain aside.

The fat guy had moved the visitor chair and Clarence was gone.

"For a second there, I thought you had left," Bob said.

I nodded. There weren't any other chairs so I wasn't sure what I was supposed to do now. Then I saw it. Five lines on some newspaper and the little fat guy grinnin' like he'd discovered his dick. He'd rolled up a dollar bill and held it out to me. I looked at the little fat guy. He gave me a side glance. Like he was shy or hiding or something.

"You're gorgeous," he said. "Come here, take a snort, huh. Show me how it's done. Make me feel at home."

I took the rolled dollar bill.

"Kneel, baby," Bob said.

He kept that frozen grin on his face. If I'd had a gun I would have shot it off there and then. I knelt down and the desk came up to my chin. So I couldn't stay kneeled or I wouldn't be able to snort the blow. I kind of crouched. I snorted a line, wiped my nose, and licked my fingers and then automatically handed him the rolled up dollar.

Bob took it real careful and put it at the edge of one of the lines. Then, like it was his first time, he snorted the line real slowly. He looked up at me, wiped his nose with his fingers and licked off the rest of the powder. Mimicking me. Maybe he was trying to make me feel at home and maybe he was playing me, I couldn't tell yet.

Then he took a bottle of Jim Beam and two shot glasses out of his briefcase lying next to the chair and put them on the table. He poured two shots and handed me one. I took a sip. I knew I shouldn't. I knew that was going to be the end. Then he did something I really didn't expect. He took out his wallet and handed me five hundred dollars. In hundred dollar bills. I took them. I folded them and put them in my purse. Now I knew that purse wasn't going out of my sight. Jeez, that amounted to three weeks work, minus the tips. I usually get pretty good tips.

Jeez, oh jeez I was happy. I smiled at him. I felt like he'd given me a million dollars in cash. Ma would be out of her mind with glee, man. I make ten dollars an hour and if I get shitty tips, the whole week's ruined.

I took another sip of the Jim Beam. The bourbon was going down good. I was feeling that buzz that usually meant I was lightening up. I forgot the little fat guy was even there. He put his paw on my ass. I shook it off without thinking. Creep.

I looked down at the little fat guy taking up the entire chair with his bulk. He just kept looking at me. I pulled my hair forward so I'd look like a blond Indian princess in that stupid off the shoulder top with my hair falling down to my waist. I leaned over and blew in the little fat guy's ear. I was beginning to feel frisky. I was feeling real 'frisky.'

The little fat guy looked up at me and for the first time I could see his eyes didn't match. I started laughing, like I was having a ball, but I was really laughing because his eyes turned outward. One eye looked out one way; the other looked out the other way. I thought he was from a Steven Spielberg sci-fi movie or something. Close Encounters of the Weirdo Kind. The guy didn't know what I was laughing at so he started laughing, too. There were two lines of coke left and I scraped up one. He did the other.

Then I sat on his lap and put my arms around his neck. Things were getting a little blurry, but I was feeling warm and that buzz-click I get on shit was working kicked in big time. I could feel he was hard. And he was sweating.

I wasn't supposed to be driving. I wasn't sure how I was going to get home. I knew it was a one-time thing, though. I told myself I'd be back in an AA meeting tomorrow and just say I slipped. Everyone slips. Keep coming back. That's the motto.

"I'd like to take you out tonight," the little fat guy says to me. "Give you a good time."

"Why can't we have a good time right here?" I ask.

"There's no room, here," he says. "I have a big Mercedes 500 outside."

"Oh, yeah," I say, starting to feel real mouthy. "You got a driver, too, I guess."

"No, I let him off for tonight."

"Oh, yeah? That was real nice of you," I said, and then I just kissed him on the mouth. I opened his lips with my tongue just lightly and smoothed the kiss off. I wiped his lips with my forefinger in case I got lipstick on them. My hair was flowing over his face. He pushed it behind my ear.

Then he gets up with me in his lap. He puts me down. He comes up to the middle of my chest, I swear. But I can see in the dim red light that he is wearing an expensive suit. His tie tack looks like real gold. He looked expensive. Small, but expensive. I swore tomorrow I'd hit a meeting. In fact, I'd even do two of 'em, AA and Narcanon.

He put his hand under my arm and led me out the back door. I swayed into the parking lot, and just like he said, I couldn't believe it, there was a big ol black four door shiny Mercedes. No other cars in the lot. He took me over to it and opened the driver's side door.

"Why don't you drive, sweetheart," he says to me.

"Look, I'd love to, but I can't drive when I'm high like this. I had to sign a contract with my PO that I'd never drive when I had something to drink," I said.

"You signed that, huh?" He said, nuzzling into my chest. He was making me sick. Men always thought they could manhandle you just 'cause they had money. He unhooked the bustier in the back, pulled it down enough to nuzzle my cleavage.

"I'm a pretty important politician around here. If anybody bothers you about driving tonight, I'm going to get you off, what do you think about that?"

He'd pulled the bustier clean off and shoved it into my purse. I was worried about the money. I didn't have a wallet. I had just folded it and put it in there. The purse was huge with a top zipper. I felt it with my hand. He'd zipped it up. That was nice. He was sucking on my left boob. I pushed his face away real gentle and pulled the pea coat over myself. He slid his hand up my thigh. I pushed his hand away.

"I'm just a little tipsy," he said in his low, creamy voice. "I don't want to drive like that. You drive, baby. Just down the freeway to this great hotel I know in Newport. It's got a view of the harbor and in the morning we'll have their Sunday brunch. Would you like that?"

I don't know why, but I thought about my little kid—my boy. That's just how I lost custody the last time. Trusting his stupid father. "Just down the freeway," Tim, my ex, had said. I'd do anything for Tim. He was six two with blond hair and he worked out at the gym everyday. Even in prison he used the gym. He had respect for his body. But the last time I was with him I was driving and some cop pulled us over and did the breathalyzer test and all that crap and I'm the one that gets busted.

Five years, one inside and four on probation and then I take this stupid, dumb, ridiculous drunk driving class in rehab and all anybody did in there was play cards and when we went back to our rooms we drank. And somebody snuck a lot of drugs in there. I just smoked the pot. It calmed me down.

When I got out of that rehab, the judge made me promise not to drink and drive again. But Tim got me drinking Southern Comfort and sure enough I get busted again, and that's when all hell broke loose, they took our son away from me and he got put up for adoption, which now I'm grateful for, and I get this song and dance and the judge and lawyers and my sponsor all got me signing some contract that if it happens a third time and anybody gets hurt, I get twenty-five to life in a penitentiary. What a crock. I have an addiction.

I got in the driver's side of the Mercedes. I've never even been in one, much less driven one. It was nice. Tan leather bucket seats.

A gorgeous wood panel, all the radio and CD stuff. A big console separating the seats to hold drinks and your stuff. Man. It was beautiful. The steering wheel was made of wood. Polished wood.

The fool gets into the passenger seat and smiles at me. His eyes smiled, too. Individually, of course. I muffled a laugh. I didn't want to hurt his feelings.

"Let's not put on the seatbelts," he says. "You're a good driver, aren't ya?"

"Gee," I said, real sarcastic. "Why no seatbelts? We gonna have fun?"

He showed me how to start the thing. Push a button. I pushed the button. The engine made a low roar, a rumbling. It sounded like the Indy 500. I put it in drive. He put his arm up and opened the sun roof. The sky was really black. No stars. The moon showed bright through the hole of the roof. It was beautiful.

I could feel the fuzziness in my head subside slightly, so I knew I could drive. No problem. We weren't going that far. I turned left out of the parking lot onto the two lane street. In the 'burbs there's never enough street lights. No cars were coming in the opposite direction though. The bright blue clock on the panel said one fifteen. Boy it gets late fast.

He put his paw on my leg again. This time I didn't push it off. Tim used to do that. He loved to rub my upper leg back and forth. It was supposed to get me hot. It didn't. I just hate people pawing me. I stared out the windshield. The houses on either side were little one-story bungalows jammed together. I heard a dog barking from somewhere in the neighborhood, but not close. If he'd been close I would have slowed down. I'd hate to run over a dog. I'd never forgive myself.

The little fat guy pinched my boob. On the outside. I would have pulled over if he'd put his paw underneath my shirt. Not while I'm driving.

A black sign, which was probably green in the daytime, said the interstate was just up ahead. I got on the ramp and blew the red light. My head was feeling really watery now. I felt like laughing, but I was also getting a little paranoid wonderin' what this guy was expecting. I don't do kink of any kind. He pulled out a flask from that expensive suit and shoved the open bottle under my right arm and right into my nose. I took the flask and took a long slurp. I kept my eyes on the highway. Then he pulled the flask out of my hand and I could hear him slurp. Two slurps and then it must have been empty because I could hear him screw on the little cap and put it under the seat.

Tim always had booze in the car. I get blamed and Tim was the one with the booze. Probably 'cause I'm a woman. After my boy was adopted out, Tim felt safer. He made love to me more than he ever had before I had the kid. He said he wasn't sure he could make love to a woman who'd given birth.

Bright lights were coming at me from the other side of the freeway and I slowed. My head was spinning and I felt like throwing up. I prayed I wouldn't. Clarence would fire my ass for sure if I fucked up this trick. The fat little guy's talking real low with that mellow voice he's got, but I swear to God I have no idea what he's saying and I can't really hear him good anyway because I'm feeling so high.

The Mercedes must have been swerving because somebody honked and yelled out the window at me. I was hoping it wasn't a gang or something. There's drive-by shootings in L.A. I smiled and gave the person a thumb's up. Real nice. Then I burped. I hear the fat little guy laughing. At me. Now he probably thinks I will do anything for him 'cause he's got me driving his big, black, fancy Mercedes. He's so rich and powerful. Oh, lucky me. I should have gotten a thousand dollars for this gig. Why did I accept five hundred?

My mouth tastes funny. Dry and sticky inside. My breath must stink. I love it. Good. I hope my breath stinks. That made me smile. The fat little guy must have thought I found whatever he was jawing about funny, cause he leaned into me, put my hand on his crotch, pulled my head back and started really kissing my cheeks and my hair, saying some more shit about how great I am.

I pull my hand away. The hard-on's gone. I kind of push him back and he gets nasty. I mean real nasty. He slaps me up the side of my head and I see stars and bright shards of light. That mixed with the booze and the coke, I'm really feeling sick. My lane is clear, though. I'm in the middle lane. No cars jammin' in front of me. Down the road I see a truck, it looked like a Fedex truck on the shoulder of the freeway. I can never tell how many feet or yards something is.

I change into the slow lane. I hear him yellin' at me, but I swear I can't hear what he's saying. Something about it being too soon to get into the lane. My head was spinning and the front of the car looked longer than I knew it probably really was. Like it was stretched out too far in front. The bumper felt like it was twenty feet long and the lights from the freeway began to blur into one really bright white light. It was hurting my eyes.

I feel him grab my hair again. Tim used to grab my hair. I push his hand away. I hear someone yelling. I realize it's me. I don't know what I'm saying, but somehow my mind takes me back to the ambulance speeding down the freeway to the hospital to deliver my son. I can hear myself calling out for Tim. I'm beginning to feel like I did then, when they took me to the emergency room. When the baby was coming too early.

The little fat guy pulls my head down to his lap and I feel his flesh. I'm gonna throw up, but I try to swallow it back. I'm really feeling sick and the car's swerving back and forth not helping matters at all. I can hear cars honking, lots of honking in the distance. I pull my head back up and we're practically on top of the Fedex truck. It came up so quick. I look over at the little fat guy and he's got this mean look on his face. I figure I'm in for a beating.

The Fedex truck is like real close on the shoulder of the freeway. I can't see anybody in it. I slam my foot on the gas as hard as I can and swerve the car toward the truck. I hear the fat guy yelling, but he sounds far away. The passenger side of the Mercedes smashes right into the back of the van. The car is practically cut in half long-wise. The car slams to a stop. I'm okay. I smell smoke and I look over at the fat guy. He's bleeding from the top of his head down his shirt. Lots of blood and white stuff gushing out and his left eye is open and wandering. He's making little jerky movements. He's not making any sounds. Fire has started on his side of the car. I was thinking the front panel with all that wood will really light up. I look up to the sun roof and it's puckered, but completely open. Like a woman's lips when she's angry. I lift my hand and see they're dirty with soot.

Bright orange and yellow flames are shooting straight up in the air from this dark, black hole that is the Mercedes and I hear voices outside. Someone must have called an ambulance and the fire department. Fire trucks and flashing colored lights surround us and somebody's yelling into a bull horn.

I'm worried about my purse. My money. It had fallen into the little fat guy's lap, but I can't get to his lap. The sun roof is sizzling, like a steak on a grill. Then I realized it wasn't the metal of the sun roof, it was my seat belt, hanging at the side by my door. I put my hand up and felt the sun roof. The opening was hot, but not that bad. The interior of the car was beginning to fill up with smoke. I got scared that pretty soon, I wouldn't be able to see the sun roof opening. I lifted myself up and stretched through the top opening onto the roof.

I didn't have to strain too hard because someone was on top of the car dressed like a ninja and grabbed my hands and pulled me through the opening. I started laughing. I was laughing as hard as I could. My saviors, my rescuers. Dribble was falling out of my mouth and I was handed down to some other big guy who put me on a white stretcher and belted me in. Tears were falling down the sides of my cheeks, but I knew I wasn't crying. I was laughing too hard.

I heard a far away voice, "This guy's dead, Lou."

I laughed even harder. I wasn't laughing at that, I just couldn't seem to stop laughing in general. Like something in my head triggered a laughing gene or something.

I was lifted into the back of the ambulance. This one looked different from the one they put me in when I was delivering my son. It had more stuff. Somebody jammed an IV needle in my arm and told me to hang in there I was going to be all right. It didn't hurt. I hate needles, but I didn't even feel this. The drugs were probably making me immune to pain or something.

The ambulance took off and I could feel us going real fast down the freeway, sirens shrieking, just like last time. I closed my eyes. I saw Tim comin' into emergency and then the two of us in my private room in the hospital. Nurses looking real sad. The dumb intern on duty looking real sad. The intern told me my son had been born dead and why didn't I have prenatal care. I started crying. And now I could feel myself crying in this ambulance.

"You're going to be okay, miss. Some scratches. You're lucky. Were you guys drinkin'?" The ambulance guy asked.

I just kept crying. I was still back at the hospital long ago and I could feel my dead baby in my arms. The nurses said it was important to say 'goodbye' to a stillborn. Tim was sitting with me, his arm around my shoulder. We were looking at my son. We were crying. We looked at his scrunched up little face. They'd put a blue cap on his head and wrapped him in a blue blanket with a lighter blue trim like they were keeping him warm. I loved Tim at that moment. We were a family. A real family. I would have brought him up good. I would have worked somewhere and made sure he went to good schools and then he'd get into a good college. I would have turned around. I would have turned my whole life around for him. But he was dead. The nurse came in and took him from my arms. And then it was just Tim and me.

"I can't do this no more, baby," Tim said, getting off the bed. "I'm sorry."

He left and then nobody was there. My first son hadn't even been Tim's. I don't know whose he was. I just put him up for adoption. My mother came to get me in a couple of days. I went to live with her until I got arrested the second time for drunk driving. I spent some time inside and then got the two rehabs which were, as I say, bullshit. I signed the paper, the contract. I wouldn't drink and drive because a third time they'd throw away the key.

I opened my eyes. Some guy maybe twenty-three, was looking at me.

"You okay?"

"Oh, yeah, I couldn't be better. You got some water?"

"I'm not supposed to give you anything to drink in case you need surgery," he says.

I turn away from him. We arrive at the emergency entry fast. They cart me off the back of the truck like I'm cold beer ready to get into a bar vat. No one is there to greet me except an ER nurse. She hooks me up to the monitors and other shit I've seen before. Then I have a full panic attack.

Did they get my purse out of there?"

"Everything's burned up far as I know," the ambulance guy says. "Cops want to talk to you."

"No," I say.

Two uniforms come in with a guy in a tan overcoat with a stupid badge pinned to the pocket.

"Miss Jillrith?"

"Jillian." I say.

Tan coat reads his notes. He crosses something out on his pad. "Miss Jillian? I'm detective Robert Hoyle. Can you tell us what happened tonight?"

He stands by the bed, holding on to the rail they put up sos I wouldn't fall out.

"Yeah, I hit a van." I said.

"Were you ever unconscious?" Tan coat asks.

"If I were unconscious I wouldn't know, now would I?" I say.

My head's beginning to beat pretty bad, but I want to get this over with. The nurse comes in and stands on the other side, checks out the drip, twirls it a little, nods at the dicks and leaves.

"Your passenger was Robert Willfield, the city councilman. He was up for re-election next year. You know him?"

"He was a date tonight," I said. "My boss at the bar where I work fixed us up."

"He was married with three children, ma'am," Tan coat says.

"Yeah, so what's he doing out with me?" I say. But now my lips feel parched again and I feel that salty wet so I know they're probably bleeding.

"I think she's had enough for right now, gentlemen," the nurse says.

Tan coat nods. "When can we interview her?"

"Let me find out." The nurse leaves again.

I lie there. I'm thinking about my purse, all that money—burned up.

An old guy comes in with another badge. This is my third hit. That's it for me. I can just see 'em gloating. Judges love to teach you a lesson. I decide then and there to tell them the truth.

"Hey, detective? The councilman pushed my head into his lap. That's when the car like veered off and hit the van. It was an accident. That's my story for the news."

The dick smiles. The nurse comes back.

"There's a tall, blond, good-looking guy in the waiting area. Tim," he says. "Says you'll want to see him. And your mother called."

Tim's here? I felt warm and happy all over. All I can think about is now is I'll get Tim to buy something for my second son on his birthday. The adopted parents would like that. Tim'll do that much for me.

✗

OUTBURSTS OF EVERETT TRUE

ANACONDA, MONTANA

by Bruce Kilstein

ANACONDA, MONTANA 1905

From the name, one would never know that it was a boomtown. When Mr. Daly set up the smelter and realized efficient ways to wring the ore from the hills, the town swelled from an ashen three hundred to a glinting nine thousand souls. The name, Copperopolis, seemed to fit the new century like a cog in the mechanism of progress, but when the postmaster found that the name was already taken, he suggested *Anaconda*. Nobody asked him why, and because they had better things to fret over, nobody suggested an alternative—the name stuck.

Montana was as good a place as any, Bridget supposed—certainly better than the Ireland she had escaped, and as nice as Pennsylvania or Massachusetts. Although constantly moving downhill (she had been sent down from the posh neighborhood where she worked for a prominent lawyer to serve a miserable businessman and his ugly daughters) she had seen enough of the eastern part of America—the hatred of the Catholics (although the Portuguese had it worse than the Irish), the oppression of servants, the gossip, the drudgery, the cruelty of the local politicians and their policemen—she had grown tired of being the dregs in the "Melting Pot," and had found a husband and moved west. When she thought about it, having a husband was like being a maid for two households but Mr. Sullivan was nice enough, the money she had was enough to get them set up in Montana (although, how could you put a price on the services she had rendered? The money may have been coined silver but the color was still red.). She supposed she could have bargained a higher severance pay but thought better of the risk; best to take what was offered and just go to a place where you could start over and, so long as you worshiped the Gods of Molten Metal, you could pray in any church you pleased. The bottom of the Pinter Mountains was better than bottom of the hill in Fall River even if the smoke stacks that towered over the town seemed a constant black finger pointing accusation.

Bridget was tired. The day's work at Mr. Winston's house complete, she went home and set about her own chores before starting dinner. The stove was cold and there would be no time for a coal fire. She went out back for wood. The August sun was still hot in early evening. She was getting no younger. Wiping the sweat from her face, she headed to the small wood pile and considered the sense in changing her style of dress to one of the lighter cotton blouses and trousers the "New Women" were wearing. She could probably afford some new clothes; but, truth be told, she was used to working in a dress and whale bone and just couldn't see herself in something so loose and stylish. It was strange enough getting used to modern conveniences (which weren't all that new, but her former employer, although a wealthy man, refused them, preferring to wander in the dark with a kerosene lamp like some tormented ghost). Now you had electric instead of gas light. (She didn't trust the stuff. Who knew what evil came though wires?) Same for telephones. Who would they call? Pshaw! The operators were always listening in and sharing your news with town busybodies. She would make proper visits to friends in town and write proper correspondence back East.

She did enjoy having a water closet.

Mr. Andrew had running water in Fall River but had it shut off to all outlets except the kitchen sink. Pennies saved. What did it get him? She shuddered when she thought of his black figure, neatly dressed for a day at the bank, bent over that sink brushing the stringy mutton from his teeth after dinner. The sound grated on her memory. The heat, the memory, the bleating of her neighbor's sheep overcame her with a wave of nausea.

That mutton. Her allowance of four dollars a week for shopping and household expenses had been more than ample, but Mr. Andrew had insisted on bargain cuts of mutton or pork—whatever was on sale that the butcher was desperate to get rid of at four cents a pound before the meat went completely rancid. She remembered cooking in that August heat wave. A generous helping of spice in the stew had masked some of the strange aftertaste but Mr. Andrew insisted that leftovers not go to waste. The ice in the box, which barely kept food at room temperature on good days, had rapidly melted; serving the remainder of the stew at breakfast the next day was ill-advised. Have mercy!

The vomiting that ensued after that cursed meal caused Mr. Andrew, Mrs. Abby and the daughter to hallucinate plots of poison. Missus ran across to fetch Dr. Brown, heaving the last of the meal on the poor man's lawn. He offered a bromide, assuring her that if it had been cyanide rather than food poisoning, she would not have had time to call on him. He accompanied her back to assist the rest of the household but was barred entry to the house and refused compensation by an irate Andrew.

Bridget paused at the woodpile. How odd that memory could be so instantly triggered. She had fought for years to suppress the recollection of that day. She selected a few logs from the pile and brought them to the stump. She cast an evil eye at the staring sheep over the fence. There were no neighbors about. The women were indoors waiting for the distant whistle that sent the men down the mountain and home from the inferno of the smelter where a cool limeade and kind word awaited. She rolled up her sleeves. The heat rose in a wave shimmering off the ground.

The heat. She had only tasted the mutton and so was less sick than the others. All were behaving badly—there had been arguments for days—heated words between Mrs. Abby and Uncle John, heated words between sister Emma and Mr. Andrew (at least Emma had the good sense to storm out a few days earlier to visit friends on the seacoast, thereby missing the stew) and, she remembered thinking but was too embarrassed to confess to Father Riley (Jesus forgive her) that she had wished it were poison when the dirty windows became a priority and she was made to wash them inside and out in the sweltering August heat. By some miracle she felt better after throwing up in the yard and so dutifully continued to the barn for a pail of water and a large pole to reach the high windows where the fresh air held a bit of breeze and was better than the stagnant interior of the house. She could chat with the neighbor's maid while she worked.

Those days seemed so long ago. She never spoke of them, not even to her husband. Mr. Sullivan asked few questions, bless him, and as she was not what any would call handsome, and had come with a considerable sum of money, he had not pursued a line of inquiry. Fortunately there was a need for domestic workers in the expanding town, and her employer had not asked for references. She sat on the stump a moment to rest. Memories revolved in her mind, turning her stomach.

The house was blessedly quiet. Emma and Uncle John had stormed off. Mr. Andrew was off to business, Mrs. Abby would be on the second floor changing the linen—she had forbidden Bridget to work on the floor where the family slept since the day money and trolley tickets had gone missing. Given the fact that everyone knew the daughter was a kleptomaniac, maybe they needed a cover story. Bridget didn't care; at least she still had a job. In some small way she pitied the girl. Having such little access to her father's money must have been a frustration. Bridget had considered a trip to the fabric store for a sale but after her chores she just wanted to lie down for an hour before having to prepare dinner. She doubted anyone would have much of an appetite anyway.

Bridget rose reluctantly and yanked the hatchet out of the stump. It made a thick, sucking sound. She turned the stained, rusted blade over in the sun imagining she could see her reflection in the dull metal.

She had finished the windows, had a drink of water, vomited again, felt a bit better, and went to her third-floor attic room to rest. She must have drifted off but awoke to strange sounds and a brief muffled shout that she assumed was the resumption of the argument between stepmother and daughter. She rolled over and tried to ignore the bickering for a few minutes and put the hot pillow over her head. The heat would not permit sleep but she stayed in bed as long as possible. When she heard Mr. Andrew's voice she realized that she had to begin cooking. She washed her face in the basin and headed downstairs. Voices came from the first floor, and on the second floor landing something made her stop dead—

Bridget placed the log on the chopping stump, lifted the axe, and paused. A sharp pain overcame her. She pinched the bridge of her nose as if to slow a bleeding memory from flowing out for the world to see—she had never told anyone and each week at the confessional she felt as if another shovelful of earth was lifted from her deepening grave. She just couldn't do it. She knew it was a sin to keep this inside her but what difference would confessing make now?

—A pair of legs protruded from the side of the bed Mrs. Abby had been changing. A red stain splattered the clean white blanket. She froze in terror. Another hurried sound came from below. Afraid to enter the bedroom, she followed the sound down the creaking stairs to the parlor.

Punishment would surely come. She had killed no one but committed a heinous sin of omission in her money-bought silence. The heat of the day would be nothing compared to the fires that awaited her.

Lizzie Borden was finishing caving in the skull of her father when Bridget entered the room. He must have died after the first few whacks but Lizzie continued on for several moments—each stroke of the axe releasing blood which splashed with the music of severed chains. The blood splattered high on the wall and pooled on the floor by the sofa where he had reclined for a nap. Lizzie, sensing Bridget behind her, turned, and with a disturbing lack of emotion, began delivering calculated instructions:

"There's no time, Maggie." All Irish maids were called that, Bridget wondered if they even knew her name. "Quickly! Fetch my pink dress and a new pair of hose." She wiped the slick fluid from the hatchet onto her blue dress and handed the weapon to Bridget.

In shock, distraught, but shamefully feeling no remorse at the death of her cruel master, Bridget took the axe, went through the kitchen, pausing to stash the instrument of murder in an unused section of the stove, and ran upstairs to find Lizzie's dress.

Lizzie changed her clothes calmly. "You will say nothing, Maggie. You were asleep upstairs when Father was killed and washing windows with witnesses when Mrs. Borden met her end. They will entertain you as a suspect but there will be no evidence. I will be tried for the murder. You will be paid well.

Before Bridget could even formulate a response—the horrible image froze in her mind, the cold horror of Lizzie's calculated plan—Lizzie was out the door calling for a doctor and the police.

Bridget's mind flashed back to the awful scene. Waves of heat, of nausea, of guilt—guilt of keeping silent, guilt of accepting money, most of all, guilt that she was happy to see Andrew and Abby Borden dead—came over her, and she moved the log off the block, set down her own left hand in its place, and raised the hatchet.

On August 4, 1892, Andrew and Abby Borden were found brutally butchered in their home. The doors to the Borden house were locked from the inside. Lizzie Borden and her maid, Bridget Sullivan, were the only other people at home. Lizzie Borden stood trial for the murders and was quickly acquitted. Forensic analysis established that Lizzie's stepmother, Abby, had died before Andrew, and so, in the mysterious absence of Andrew Borden's will, his large estate went to Lizzie. Many officials were handsomely paid from this purse. Lizzie lived comfortably for the remainder of her life in Fall River, Massachusetts, just a few blocks from the murder. Bridget Sullivan, the only possible witness to the crime, died in 1948 in Montana. She never spoke of that horrible day.

✗

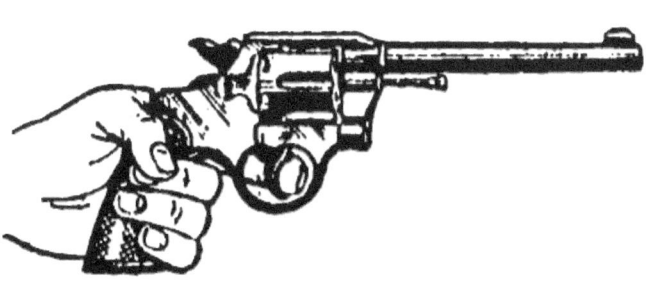

THE MAN WITH THE TWISTED LIP

by Sir Arthur Conan Doyle

Isa Whitney, brother of the late Elias Whitney, DD, Principal of the Theological College of St George's, was much addicted to opium. The habit grew upon him, as I understand, from some foolish freak when he was at college; for having read De Quincey's description of his dreams and sensations, he had drenched his tobacco with laudanum in an attempt to produce the same effects. He found, as so many more have done, that the practice is easier to attain than to get rid of, and for many years he continued to be a slave to the drug, an object of mingled horror and pity to his friends and relatives. I can see him now, with yellow, pasty face, drooping lids, and pin-point pupils, all huddled in a chair, the wreck and ruin of a noble man.

One night—it was in June, '89—there came a ring to my bell, about the hour when a man gives his first yawn and glances at the clock. I sat up in my chair, and my wife laid her needle-work down in her lap and made a little face of disappointment.

"A patient!" said she. "You'll have to go out."

I groaned, for I was newly come back from a weary day.

We heard the door open, a few hurried words, and then quick steps upon the linoleum. Our own door flew open, and a lady, clad in some dark-coloured stuff,

with a black veil, entered the room.

"You will excuse my calling so late," she began, and then, suddenly losing her self-control, she ran forward, threw her arms about my wife's neck, and sobbed upon her shoulder. "Oh, I'm in such trouble!" she cried; "I do so want a little help."

"Why," said my wife, pulling up her veil, "it is Kate Whitney. How you startled me, Kate! I had not an idea who you were when you came in."

"I didn't know what to do, so I came straight to you." That was always the way. Folk who were in grief came to my wife like birds to a light-house.

"It was very sweet of you to come. Now, you must have some wine and water, and sit here comfortably and tell us all about it. Or should you rather that I sent James off to bed?"

"Oh, no, no! I want the doctor's advice and help, too. It's about Isa. He has not been home for two days. I am so frightened about him!"

It was not the first time that she had spoken to us of her husband's trouble, to me as a doctor, to my wife as an old friend and school companion. We soothed and comforted her by such words as we could find. Did she know where her husband was? Was it possible that we could bring him back to her?

It seems that it was. She had the surest information that of late he had, when the fit was on him, made use of an opium den in the farthest east of the City. Hitherto his orgies had always been confined to one day, and he had come back, twitching and shattered, in the evening. But now the spell had been upon him eight-and-forty hours, and he lay there, doubtless among the dregs of the docks, breathing in the poison or sleeping off the effects. There he was to be found, she was sure of it, at the Bar of Gold, in Upper Swandam Lane. But what was she to do? How could she, a young and timid woman, make her way into such a place and pluck her husband out from among the ruffians who surrounded him?

There was the case, and of course there was but one way out of it. Might I not escort her to this place? And then, as a second thought, why should she come at all? I was Isa Whitney's medical adviser, and as such I had influence over him. I could manage it better if I were alone. I promised her on my word that I would send him home in a cab within two hours if he were indeed at the address which she had given me. And so in ten minutes I had left my armchair and cheery sitting-room behind me, and was speeding eastward in a hansom on a strange errand, as it seemed to me at the time, though the future only could show how strange it was to be.

But there was no great difficulty in the first stage of my adventure. Upper Swandam Lane is a vile alley lurking behind the high wharves which line the north side of the river to the east of London Bridge. Between a slop-shop and a gin-shop, approached by a steep flight of steps leading down to a black gap like the mouth of a cave, I found the den of which I was in search. Ordering my cab to wait, I passed down the steps, worn hollow in the centre by the ceaseless tread of drunken feet; and by the light of a flickering oil-lamp above the door I found the latch and made my way into a long, low room, thick and heavy with brown opium smoke, and terraced with wooden berths, like the forecastle of an emigrant ship.

Through the gloom one could dimly catch a glimpse of bodies lying in strange fantastic poses, bowed shoulders, bent knees, heads thrown back, and chins pointing upward, with here and there a dark, lack-lustre eye turned upon the newcomer. Out of the black shadows there glimmered little red circles of light, now bright, now faint, as the burning poison waxed or waned in the bowls of the metal pipes. The most lay silent, but some muttered to themselves, and others talked together in a strange, low, monotonous voice, their conversation coming in gushes, and then suddenly tailing off into silence, each mumbling out his own thoughts and paying little heed to the words of his neighbour. At the farther end was a small brazier of burning charcoal, beside which on a three-legged wooden stool there sat a tall, thin old man, with his jaw resting upon his two fists, and his elbows upon his knees, staring into the fire.

As I entered, a sallow Malay attendant had hurried up with a pipe for me and a supply of the drug, beckoning me to an empty berth.

"Thank you. I have not come to stay," said I. "There is a friend of mine here, Mr Isa Whitney, and I wish to speak with him."

There was a movement and an exclamation from my right, and peering through the gloom, I saw Whitney, pale, haggard, and unkempt, staring out at me.

"My God! It's Watson," said he. He was in a pitiable state of reaction, with every nerve in a twitter. "I say, Watson, what o'clock is it?"

"Nearly eleven."

"Of what day?"

"Of Friday, June 19th."

"Good heavens! I thought it was Wednesday. It is Wednesday. What d'you want to frighten a chap for?" He sank his face onto his arms and began to sob in a high treble key.

"I tell you that it is Friday, man. Your wife has been waiting this two days for you. You should be ashamed of yourself!"

"So I am. But you've got mixed, Watson, for I have only been here a few hours, three pipes, four pipes—I forget how many. But I'll go home with you. I wouldn't frighten Kate—poor little Kate. Give me your hand! Have you a cab?"

"Yes, I have one waiting."

"Then I shall go in it. But I must owe something. Find what I owe, Watson. I am all off colour. I can do nothing for myself."

I walked down the narrow passage between the double row of sleepers, holding my breath to keep out the vile, stupefying fumes of the drug, and looking about for the manager. As I passed the tall man who sat by the brazier I felt a sudden pluck at my skirt, and a low voice whispered, "Walk past me, and then look back at me." The words fell quite distinctly upon my ear. I glanced down. They could only have come from the old man at my side, and yet he sat now as absorbed as ever, very thin, very wrinkled, bent with age, an opium pipe dangling down from between his knees, as though it had dropped in sheer lassitude from his fingers. I took two steps forward and looked back. It took all my self-control to prevent me from breaking out into a cry of astonishment. He had turned his back so that none could see him but I. His form had filled out, his wrinkles were gone, the dull eyes had regained their fire, and there, sitting by the fire and grinning at my surprise, was none other than Sherlock Holmes. He made a slight motion to me to approach him, and instantly, as he turned his face half round to the company once more, subsided into a doddering, loose-lipped senility.

"Holmes!" I whispered, "what on earth are you doing in this den?"

"As low as you can," he answered; "I have excellent ears. If you would have the great kindness to get rid of that sottish friend of yours I should be exceedingly glad to have a little talk with you."

"I have a cab outside."

"Then pray send him home in it. You may safely trust him, for he appears to be too limp to get into any mischief. I should recommend you also send a note by the cabman to your wife to say that you have thrown in your lot with me. If you will wait outside, I shall be with you in five minutes."

It was difficult to refuse any of Sherlock Holmes's requests, for they were always so exceedingly definite, and put forward with such a quiet air of mastery. I felt, however, that when Whitney was once confined in the cab my mission was practically accomplished; and for the rest, I could not wish anything better than to be associated with my friend in one of those singular adventures which were the normal condition of his existence. In a few minutes I had written my note, paid Whitney's bill, led him out to the cab, and seen him driven through the darkness. In a very short time a decrepit figure emerged from the opium den, and I was walking down the street with Sherlock Holmes. For two streets he shuffled along with a bent back and an uncertain foot. Then, glancing quickly round, he straightened himself out and burst into a hearty fit of laughter.

"I suppose, Watson," said he, "that you imagine that I have added opium-smoking to cocaine injections, and all the other little weaknesses on which you have favoured me with your medical views."

"I was certainly surprised to find you there."

"But not more so than I to find you."

"I came to find a friend."

"And I to find an enemy."

"An enemy?"

"Yes; one of my natural enemies, or, shall I say, my natural prey. Briefly, Watson, I am in the midst of a very remarkable inquiry, and I have hoped to find a clue in the incoherent ramblings of these sots, as I have done before now. Had I been recognised in that den my life would not have been worth an hour's purchase; for I have used it before now for my own purposes, and the rascally Lascar who runs it has sworn to have vengeance upon me. There is a trap-door at the back of that building, near the corner of Paul's Wharf, which could tell some strange tales of what has passed through it upon the moonless nights."

"What! You do not mean bodies?"

"Ay, bodies, Watson. We should be rich men if we had 1000 pounds for every poor devil who has been done to death in that den. It is the vilest murder-trap on the whole riverside, and I fear that Neville St Clair has entered it never to leave it more. But our trap should be here." He put his two forefingers between his teeth and whistled shrilly—a signal which was answered by a similar whistle from the distance, followed shortly by the rattle of wheels and the clink of horses's hoofs.

"Now, Watson," said Holmes, as a tall dog-cart dashed up through the gloom, throwing out two golden tunnels of yellow light from its side lanterns. "You'll come with me, won't you?"

"If I can be of use."

"Oh, a trusty comrade is always of use; and a chronicler still more so. My room at The Cedars is a double-bedded one."

"The Cedars?"

"Yes; that is Mr St Clair's house. I am staying there while I conduct the inquiry."

"Where is it, then?"

"Near Lee, in Kent. We have a seven-mile drive before us."

"But I am all in the dark."

"Of course you are. You'll know all about it presently. Jump up here. All right, John; we shall not need you. Here's half a crown. Look out for me to-morrow, about eleven. Give her her head. So long, then!"

He flicked the horse with his whip, and we dashed away through the endless succession of sombre and deserted streets, which widened gradually, until we were flying across a broad balustraded bridge, with the murky river flowing sluggishly beneath us. Beyond lay another dull wilderness of bricks and mortar, its silence broken only by the heavy, regular footfall of the policeman, or the songs and shouts of some belated party of revellers. A dull wrack was drifting slowly across the sky, and a star or two twinkled dimly here and there through the rifts of the clouds. Holmes drove in silence, with his head sunk upon his breast, and the air of a man who is lost in thought, while I sat beside him, curious to learn what this new quest might be which seemed to tax his powers so sorely, and yet afraid to break in upon the current of his thoughts. We had driven several miles, and were beginning to get to the fringe of the belt of suburban villas, when he shook himself, shrugged his shoulders, and lit up his pipe with the air of a man who has satisfied himself that he is acting for the best.

"You have a grand gift of silence, Watson," said he. "It makes you quite invaluable as a companion. 'Pon my word, it is a great thing for me to have someone to talk to, for my own thoughts are not over-pleasant. I was wondering what I should say to this dear little woman to-night when she meets me at the door."

"You forget that I know nothing about it."

"I shall just have time to tell you the facts of the case before we get to Lee. It seems absurdly simple, and yet, somehow I can get nothing to go upon. There's plenty of thread, no doubt, but I can't get the end of it into my hand. Now, I'll state the case clearly and concisely to you, Watson, and maybe you can see a spark where all is dark to me."

"Proceed, then."

"Some years ago—to be definite, in May, 1884—there came to Lee a gentleman, Neville St Clair by name, who appeared to have plenty of money. He took a large villa, laid out the grounds very nicely, and lived generally in good style. By degrees he made friends in the neighbourhood, and in 1887 he married the daughter of a local brewer, by whom he now has two children. He had no occupation, but was interested in several companies and went into town as a rule in the morning, returning by the 5:14 from Cannon Street every night. Mr St Clair is now thirty-seven years of age, is a man of temperate habits, a good husband, a very affectionate father, and a man who is popular with all who know him. I may add that his whole debts at the present moment, as far as we have been able to ascertain, amount to 88 pounds 10s, while he has 220 pounds standing to his credit in the Capital and Counties Bank. There is no reason, therefore, to think that money troubles have been weighing upon his mind.

"Last Monday Mr Neville St Clair went into town rather earlier than usual, remarking before he started that he had two important commissions to perform, and that he would bring his little boy home a box of bricks. Now, by the merest chance, his wife received a telegram upon this same Monday, very shortly after his departure, to the effect that a small parcel of considerable value which she had been expecting was waiting for her at the offices of the Aberdeen Shipping Company. Now, if you are well up in your London, you will know that the office of the company is in Fresno Street, which branches out of Upper Swandam Lane, where you found me to-night. Mrs St Clair had her lunch, started for the City, did some shopping, proceeded to the company's office, got her packet, and found herself at exactly 4:35 walking through Swandam Lane on her way back to the station. Have you followed me so far?"

"It is very clear."

"If you remember, Monday was an exceedingly hot day, and Mrs St Clair walked slowly, glancing about in the hope of seeing a cab, as she did not like the neighbourhood in which she found herself. While she was walking in this way down Swandam Lane, she suddenly heard an ejaculation or cry, and was struck cold to see her husband looking down at her and, as it seemed to her, beckoning to her from a second-floor window. The window was open, and she distinctly saw his face, which she describes as being terribly agitated. He waved his hands frantically to her, and then vanished from the window so suddenly that it seemed to her that he had been plucked back by some irresistible force from behind. One singular point which struck her quick feminine eye was that although he wore some dark coat, such as he had started to town in, he had on neither collar nor necktie.

"Convinced that something was amiss with him, she rushed down the steps—for the house was none other than the opium den in which you found me to-night—and running through the front room she attempted to ascend the stairs which led to the first floor. At the foot of the stairs, however, she met this Lascar scoundrel of whom I have spoken, who thrust her back and, aided by a Dane, who acts as assistant there, pushed her out into the street. Filled with the most maddening doubts and fears, she rushed down the lane and, by rare good-fortune, met in Fresno Street a number of constables with an inspector, all on their way to their beat. The inspector and two men accompanied her back, and in spite of the continued resistance of the proprietor, they made their way to the room in which Mr St Clair had last been seen. There was no sign of him there. In fact, in the whole of that floor there was no one to be found save a crippled wretch of hideous aspect, who, it seems, made his home there. Both he and the Lascar stoutly swore that no one else had been in the front room during the afternoon. So determined was their denial that the inspector was staggered, and had almost come to believe that Mrs St Clair had been deluded when, with a cry, she sprang at a small deal box which lay upon the table and tore the lid from it. Out there fell a cascade of children's bricks. It was the toy which he had promised to bring home.

"This discovery, and the evident confusion which the cripple showed, made the inspector realise that the matter was serious. The rooms were carefully examined, and results all pointed to an abominable crime. The front room was plainly furnished as a sitting-room and led into a small bedroom, which looked out upon the back of one of the wharves. Between the wharf and the bedroom window is a narrow strip, which is dry at low tide but is covered at high tide with at least four and a half feet of water. The bedroom window was a broad one and opened from below. On examination traces of blood were to be seen upon the windowsill, and several scattered drops were visible upon the wooden floor of the bedroom. Thrust away behind a curtain in the front room were all the clothes of Mr Neville St Clair, with the exception of his coat. His boots, his socks, his hat, and his watch—all were there. There were no signs of violence upon any of these garments, and there were no other traces of Mr Neville St Clair. Out of the window he must apparently have gone for no other exit could be discovered, and the ominous bloodstains upon the sill gave little promise that he could save himself by swimming, for the tide was at its very highest at the moment of the tragedy.

"And now as to the villains who seemed to be immediately implicated in the matter. The Lascar was known to be a man of the vilest antecedents, but as, by Mrs St Clair's story, he was known to have been at the foot of the stair within a very few seconds of her husband's appearance at the window, he could hardly have been more than an accessory to the crime. His defence was one of absolute ignorance, and he protested that he had no knowledge as to the doings of Hugh Boone, his lodger, and that he could not account in any way for the presence of the missing gentleman's clothes.

"So much for the Lascar manager. Now for the sinister cripple who lives upon the second floor of the opium den, and who was certainly the last human being whose eyes rested upon Neville St Clair. His name is Hugh Boone, and his hideous face is one which is familiar to every man who goes much to the City. He is a professional beggar, though in order to avoid the police regulations he pretends to a small trade in wax vestas. Some little distance down Threadneedle Street, upon the left-hand side, there is, as you may have remarked, a small angle in the wall. Here it is that this creature takes his daily seat, cross-legged with his tiny stock of matches on his lap, and as he is a piteous spectacle a small rain of charity descends into the greasy leather cap which lies upon the pavement beside him. I have watched the fellow more than once before ever I thought of making his professional acquaintance, and I have been surprised at the harvest which he has reaped in a short time. His appearance, you see, is so remarkable that no one can pass him without observing him. A shock of orange hair, a pale face disfigured by a horrible scar, which, by its contraction, has turned up the outer edge of his upper lip, a bulldog chin, and a pair of very penetrating dark eyes, which present a singular contrast to the colour of his hair, all mark him out from amid the common crowd of mendicants and so, too, does his wit, for he is ever ready with a reply to any piece of chaff which may be thrown at him by the passers-by. This is the man whom we now learn to have been the lodger at the opium den, and to have been the last man to see the gentleman of whom we are in quest."

"But a cripple!" said I. "What could he have done single-handed against a man in the prime of life?"

"He is a cripple in the sense that he walks with a limp; but in other respects he appears to be a powerful and well-nurtured man. Surely your medical experience would tell you, Watson, that weakness in one limb is often compensated for by exceptional strength in the others."

"Pray continue your narrative."

"Mrs St Clair had fainted at the sight of the blood upon the window, and she was escorted home in a cab by the police, as her presence could be of no help to them in their investigations. Inspector Barton, who had charge of the case, made a very careful examination of the premises, but without finding anything which threw any light upon the matter. One mistake had been made in not arresting Boone instantly, as he was allowed some few minutes during which he might have communicated with his friend the Lascar, but this fault was soon remedied, and he was seized and searched, without anything being found which could incriminate him. There were, it is true, some blood-stains upon his right shirt-sleeve, but he pointed to his ring-finger, which had been cut near the nail, and explained that the bleeding came from there, adding that he had been to the window not long before, and that the stains which had been observed there came doubtless from the same source. He denied strenuously having ever seen Mr Neville St Clair and swore that the presence of the clothes in his room was as much a mystery to him as to the police. As to Mrs St Clair's assertion that she had actually seen her husband at the window, he declared that she must have been either mad or dreaming. He was removed, loudly protesting, to the police-station, while the inspector remained upon the premises in the hope that the ebbing tide might afford some fresh clue.

"And it did, though they hardly found upon the mud-bank what they had feared to find. It was Neville St Clair's coat, and not Neville St Clair, which lay uncovered as the tide receded. And what do you think they found in the pockets?"

"I cannot imagine."

"No, I don't think you would guess. Every pocket stuffed with pennies and half-pennies—421 pennies and 270 half-pennies. It was no wonder that it had not been swept away by the tide. But a human body is a different matter. There is a fierce eddy between the wharf and the house. It seemed likely enough that the weighted coat had remained when the stripped body had been sucked away into the river."

"But I understand that all the other clothes were found in the room. Would the body be dressed in a coat alone?"

"No, sir, but the facts might be met speciously enough. Suppose that this man Boone had thrust Neville St Clair through the window, there is no human eye which could have seen the deed. What would he do then? It would of course instantly strike him that he must get rid of the tell-tale garments. He would seize the coat, then, and be in the act of throwing it out, when it would occur to him that it would swim and not sink. He has little time, for he has heard the scuffle downstairs when the wife tried to force her way up, and perhaps he has already heard from his Lascar confederate that the police are hurrying up the street. There is not an instant to be lost. He rushes to some secret hoard, where he has accumulated the fruits of his beggary, and he stuffs all the coins upon which he can lay his hands into the pockets to make sure of the coat's sinking. He throws it out, and would have done the same with the other garments had not he heard the rush of steps below, and only just had time to close the window when the police appeared."

"It certainly sounds feasible."

"Well, we will take it as a working hypothesis for want of a better. Boone, as I have told you, was arrested and taken to the station, but it could not be shown that there had ever before been anything against him. He had for years been known as a professional beggar, but his life appeared to have been a very quiet and innocent one. There the matter stands at present, and the questions which have to be solved—what Neville St Clair was doing in the opium den, what happened to him when there, where is he now, and what Hugh Boone had to do with his disappearance—are all as far from a solution as ever. I confess that I cannot recall any case within my experience which looked at the first glance so simple and yet which presented such difficulties."

While Sherlock Holmes had been detailing this singular series of events, we had been whirling through the outskirts of the great town until the last straggling houses had been left behind, and we rattled along with a country hedge upon either side of us. Just as he finished, however, we drove through two scattered villages, where a few lights still glimmered in the windows.

"We are on the outskirts of Lee," said my companion. "We have touched on three English counties in our short drive, starting in Middlesex, passing over an angle of Surrey, and ending in Kent. See that light among the trees? That is The Cedars, and beside that lamp sits a woman whose anxious ears have already, I have little doubt, caught the clink of our horse's feet."

"But why are you not conducting the case from Baker Street?" I asked.

"Because there are many inquiries which must be made out here. Mrs St Clair has most kindly put two rooms at my disposal, and you may rest assured that she will have nothing but a welcome for my friend and colleague. I hate to meet her, Watson, when I have no news of her husband. Here we are. Whoa, there, whoa!"

We had pulled up in front of a large villa which stood within its own grounds. A stable-boy had run out to the horse's head, and springing down, I followed Holmes up the small, winding gravel-drive which led to the house. As we approached, the door flew open, and a little blonde woman stood in the opening, clad in some sort of light mousseline de soie, with a touch of fluffy pink chiffon at her neck and wrists. She stood with her figure outlined against the flood of light, one hand upon the door, one half-raised in her eagerness, her body slightly bent, her head and face protruded, with eager eyes and parted lips, a standing question.

"Well?" she cried, "well?" And then, seeing that there were two of us, she gave a cry of hope which sank into a groan as she saw that my companion shook his head and shrugged his shoulders.

"No good news?"

"None."

"No bad?"

"No."

"Thank God for that. But come in. You must be weary, for you have had a long day."

"This is my friend, Dr Watson. He has been of most vital use to me in several of my cases, and a lucky chance has made it possible for me to bring him out and associate him with this investigation."

"I am delighted to see you," said she, pressing my hand warmly. "You will, I am sure, forgive anything that may be wanting in our arrangements, when you consider the blow which has come so suddenly upon us."

"My dear madam," said I, "I am an old campaigner, and if I were not I can very well see that no apology is needed. If I can be of any assistance, either to you or to my friend here, I shall be indeed happy."

"Now, Mr Sherlock Holmes," said the lady as we entered a well-lit dining-room, upon the table of which a cold supper had been laid out, "I should very much like to ask you one or two plain questions, to which I beg that you will give a plain answer."

"Certainly, madam."

"Do not trouble about my feelings. I am not hysterical, nor given to fainting. I simply wish to hear your real, real opinion."

"Upon what point?"

"In your heart of hearts, do you think that Neville is alive?"

Sherlock Holmes seemed to be embarrassed by the question. "Frankly, now!" she repeated, standing upon the rug and looking keenly down at him as he leaned back in a basket-chair.

"Frankly, then, madam, I do not."

"You think that he is dead?"

"I do."

"Murdered?"

"I don't say that. Perhaps."

"And on what day did he meet his death?"

"On Monday."

"Then perhaps, Mr Holmes, you will be good enough to explain how it is that I have received a letter from him to-day."

Sherlock Holmes sprang out of his chair as if he had been galvanised.

"What!" he roared.

"Yes, to-day." She stood smiling, holding up a little slip of paper in the air.

"May I see it?"

"Certainly."

He snatched it from her in his eagerness, and smoothing it out upon the table he drew over the lamp and examined it intently. I had left my chair and was gazing at it over his shoulder. The envelope was a very coarse one and was stamped with the Gravesend postmark and with the date of that very day, or rather of the day before, for it was considerably after midnight.

"Coarse writing," murmured Holmes. "Surely this is not your husband's writing, madam."

"No, but the enclosure is."

"I perceive also that whoever addressed the envelope had to go and inquire as to the address."

"How can you tell that?"

"The name, you see, is in perfectly black ink, which has dried itself. The rest is of the greyish colour, which shows that blotting-paper has been used. If it had been written straight off, and then blotted, none would be of a deep black shade. This man has written the name, and there has then been a pause before he wrote the address, which can only mean that he was not familiar with it. It is, of course, a trifle, but there is nothing so important as trifles. Let us now see the letter. Ha! there has been an enclosure here!"

"Yes, there was a ring. His signet-ring."

"And you are sure that this is your husband's hand?"

"One of his hands."

"One?"

"His hand when he wrote hurriedly. It is very unlike his usual writing, and yet I know it well."

"'Dearest, do not be frightened. All will come well. There is a huge error which it may take some little time to rectify. Wait in patience.—NEVILLE.' Written in pencil upon the fly-leaf of a book, octavo size, no water-mark. Hum! Posted to-day in Gravesend by a man with a dirty thumb. Ha! And the flap has been gummed, if I am not very much in error, by a person who had been chewing tobacco. And you have no doubt that it is your husband's hand, madam?"

"None. Neville wrote those words."

"And they were posted to-day at Gravesend. Well, Mrs St Clair, the clouds lighten, though I should not venture to say that the danger is over."

"But he must be alive, Mr Holmes."

"Unless this is a clever forgery to put us on the wrong scent. The ring, after all, proves nothing. It may have been taken from him."

"No, no; it is, it is his very own writing!"

"Very well. It may, however, have been written on Monday and only posted to-day."

"That is possible."

"If so, much may have happened between."

"Oh, you must not discourage me, Mr Holmes. I know that all is well with him. There is so keen a sympathy between us that I should know if evil came upon him. On the very day that I saw him last he cut himself in the bedroom, and yet I in the dining-room rushed upstairs instantly with the utmost certainty that something had happened. Do you think that I would respond to such a trifle and yet be ignorant of his death?"

"I have seen too much not to know that the impression of a woman may be more valuable than the conclusion of an analytical reasoner. And in this letter you certainly have a very strong piece of evidence to corroborate your view. But if your husband is alive and able to write letters, why should he remain away from you?"

"I cannot imagine. It is unthinkable."

"And on Monday he made no remarks before leaving you?"

"No."

"And you were surprised to see him in Swandam Lane?"

"Very much so."

"Was the window open?"

"Yes."

"Then he might have called to you?"

"He might."

"He only, as I understand, gave an inarticulate cry?"

"Yes."

"A call for help, you thought?"

"Yes. He waved his hands."

"But it might have been a cry of surprise. Astonishment at the unexpected sight of you might cause him to throw up his hands?"

"It is possible."

"And you thought he was pulled back?"

"He disappeared so suddenly."

"He might have leaped back. You did not see anyone else in the room?"

"No, but this horrible man confessed to having been there, and the Lascar was at the foot of the stairs."

"Quite so. Your husband, as far as you could see, had his ordinary clothes on?"

"But without his collar or tie. I distinctly saw his bare throat."

"Had he ever spoken of Swandam Lane?"

"Never."

"Had he ever shown any signs of having taken opium?"

"Never."

"Thank you, Mrs St Clair. Those are the principal points about which I wished to be absolutely clear. We shall now have a little supper and then retire, for we may have a very busy day to-morrow."

A large and comfortable double-bedded room had been placed at our disposal, and I was quickly between the sheets, for I was weary after my night of adventure. Sherlock Holmes was a man, however, who, when he had an unsolved problem upon his mind, would go for days, and even for a week, without rest, turning it over, rearranging his facts, looking at it from every point of view until he had either fathomed it or convinced himself that his data were insufficient. It was soon evident to me that he was now preparing for an all-night sitting. He took off his coat and waistcoat, put on a large blue dressing-gown, and then wandered about the room collecting pillows from his bed and cushions from the sofa and armchairs. With these he constructed a sort of Eastern divan, upon which he perched himself cross-legged, with an ounce of shag tobacco and a box of matches laid out in front of him. In the dim light of the lamp I saw him sitting there, an old briar pipe between his lips, his eyes fixed vacantly upon the corner of the ceiling, the blue smoke curling up from him, silent, motionless, with the light shining upon his strong-set aquiline features. So he sat as I dropped off to sleep, and so he sat when a sudden ejaculation caused me to wake up, and I found the summer sun shining into the apartment. The pipe was still between his lips, the smoke still curled upward, and the room was full of a dense tobacco haze, but nothing remained of the heap of shag which I had seen upon the previous night.

"Awake, Watson?" he asked.

"Yes."

"Game for a morning drive?"

"Certainly."

"Then dress. No one is stirring yet, but I know where the stable-boy sleeps,

and we shall soon have the trap out." He chuckled to himself as he spoke, his eyes twinkled, and he seemed a different man to the sombre thinker of the previous night.

As I dressed I glanced at my watch. It was no wonder that no one was stirring. It was twenty-five minutes past four. I had hardly finished when Holmes returned with the news that the boy was putting in the horse.

"I want to test a little theory of mine," said he, pulling on his boots. "I think, Watson, that you are now standing in the presence of one of the most absolute fools in Europe. I deserve to be kicked from here to Charing Cross. But I think I have the key of the affair now."

"And where is it?" I asked, smiling.

"In the bathroom," he answered. "Oh, yes, I am not joking," he continued, seeing my look of incredulity. "I have just been there, and I have taken it out, and I have got it in this Gladstone bag. Come on, my boy, and we shall see whether it will not fit the lock."

We made our way downstairs as quietly as possible, and out into the bright morning sunshine. In the road stood our horse and trap, with the half-clad stable-boy waiting at the head. We both sprang in, and away we dashed down the London Road. A few country carts were stirring, bearing in vegetables to the metropolis, but the lines of villas on either side were as silent and lifeless as some city in a dream.

"It has been in some points a singular case," said Holmes, flicking the horse on into a gallop. "I confess that I have been as blind as a mole, but it is better to learn wisdom late than never to learn it at all."

In town the earliest risers were just beginning to look sleepily from their windows as we drove through the streets of the Surrey side. Passing down the Waterloo Bridge Road we crossed over the river, and dashing up Wellington Street wheeled sharply to the right and found ourselves in Bow Street. Sherlock Holmes was well known to the force, and the two constables at the door saluted him. One of them held the horse's head while the other led us in.

"Who is on duty?" asked Holmes.

"Inspector Bradstreet, sir."

"Ah, Bradstreet, how are you?" A tall, stout official had come down the stone-flagged passage, in a peaked cap and frogged jacket. "I wish to have a quiet word with you, Bradstreet."

"Certainly, Mr Holmes. Step into my room here." It was a small, office-like room, with a huge ledger upon the table, and a telephone projecting from the wall. The inspector sat down at his desk.

"What can I do for you, Mr Holmes?"

"I called about that beggarman, Boone—the one who was charged with being concerned in the disappearance of Mr Neville St Clair, of Lee."

"Yes. He was brought up and remanded for further inquiries."

"So I heard. You have him here?"

"In the cells."

"Is he quiet?"

"Oh, he gives no trouble. But he is a dirty scoundrel."

"Dirty?"

"Yes, it is all we can do to make him wash his hands, and his face is as black as a tinker's. Well, when once his case has been settled, he will have a regular prison bath; and I think, if you saw him, you would agree with me that he needed it."

"I should like to see him very much."

"Would you? That is easily done. Come this way. You can leave your bag."

"No, I think that I'll take it."

"Very good. Come this way, if you please." He led us down a passage, opened a barred door, passed down a winding stair, and brought us to a whitewashed corridor with a line of doors on each side.

"The third on the right is his," said the inspector. "Here it is!" He quietly shot back a panel in the upper part of the door and glanced through.

"He is asleep," said he. "You can see him very well."

We both put our eyes to the grating. The prisoner lay with his face towards us in a very deep sleep, breathing slowly and heavily. He was a middle-sized man, coarsely clad as became his calling, with a coloured shirt protruding through the rent in his tattered coat. He was, as the inspector had said, extremely dirty, but the grime which covered his face could not conceal its repulsive ugliness. A broad wheal from an old scar ran right across it from eye to chin, and by its contraction had turned up one side of the upper lip, so that three teeth were exposed in a perpetual snarl. A shock of very bright red hair grew low over his eyes and forehead.

"He's a beauty, isn't he?" said the inspector.

"He certainly needs a wash," remarked Holmes. "I had an idea that he might, and I took the liberty of bringing the tools with me." He opened the Gladstone bag as he spoke, and took out, to my astonishment, a very large bath-sponge.

"He! he! You are a funny one," chuckled the inspector.

"Now, if you will have the great goodness to open that door very quietly, we will soon make him cut a much more respectable figure."

"Well, I don't know why not," said the inspector. "He doesn't look a credit to the Bow Street cells, does he?" He slipped his key into the lock, and we all very quietly entered the cell. The sleeper half turned, and then settled down once more into a deep slumber. Holmes stooped to the water-jug, moistened his sponge, and then rubbed it twice vigorously across and down the prisoner's face.

"Let me introduce you," he shouted, "to Mr Neville St Clair, of Lee, in the county of Kent."

Never in my life have I seen such a sight. The man's face peeled off under the sponge like the bark from a tree. Gone was the coarse brown tint! Gone, too, was the horrid scar which had seamed it across, and the twisted lip which had given the repulsive sneer to the face! A twitch brought away the tangled red hair, and there, sitting up in his bed, was a pale, sad-faced, refined-looking man, black-haired and smooth-skinned, rubbing his eyes and staring about him with sleepy bewilderment. Then suddenly realising the exposure, he broke into a scream and threw himself down with his face to the pillow.

"Great heavens!" cried the inspector, "it is, indeed, the missing man. I know him from the photograph."

The prisoner turned with the reckless air of a man who abandons himself to his destiny. "Be it so," said he. "And pray what am I charged with?"

"With making away with Mr Neville St— Oh, come, you can't be charged with that unless they make a case of attempted suicide of it," said the inspector with a grin. "Well, I have been twenty-seven years in the force, but this really takes the cake."

"If I am Mr Neville St Clair, then it is obvious that no crime has been committed, and that, therefore, I am illegally detained."

"No crime, but a very great error has been committed," said Holmes. "You would have done better to have trusted you wife."

"It was not the wife; it was the children," groaned the prisoner. "God help me, I would not have them ashamed of their father. My God! What an exposure! What can I do?"

Sherlock Holmes sat down beside him on the couch and patted him kindly on the shoulder.

"If you leave it to a court of law to clear the matter up," said he, "of course you can hardly avoid publicity. On the other hand, if you convince the police authorities that there is no possible case against you, I do not know that there is any reason that the details should find their way into the papers. Inspector Bradstreet would, I am sure, make notes upon anything which you might tell us and submit it to the proper authorities. The case would then never go into court at all."

"God bless you!" cried the prisoner passionately. "I would have endured imprisonment, ay, even execution, rather than have left my miserable secret as a family blot to my children.

"You are the first who have ever heard my story. My father was a schoolmaster in Chesterfield, where I received an excellent education. I travelled in my youth, took to the stage, and finally became a reporter on an evening paper in London. One day my editor wished to have a series of articles upon begging in the metropolis, and I volunteered to supply them. There was the point from which all my adventures started. It was only by trying begging as an amateur that I could get the facts upon which to base my articles. When an actor I had, of course, learned all the secrets of making up, and had been famous in the green-room for my skill. I took advantage now of my attainments. I painted my face, and to make myself as pitiable as possible I made a good scar and fixed one side of my lip in a twist by the aid of a small slip of flesh-coloured plaster. Then with a red head of hair, and an appropriate dress, I took my station in the business part of the city, ostensibly as a match-seller but really as a beggar. For seven hours I plied my trade, and when I returned home in the evening I found to my surprise that I had received no less than 26s 4d.

"I wrote my articles and thought little more of the matter until, some time later, I backed a bill for a friend and had a writ served upon me for 25 pounds. I was at my wit's end where to get the money, but a sudden idea came to me. I begged a fortnight's grace from the creditor, asked for a holiday from my employers, and spent the time in begging in the City under my disguise. In ten days I had the money and paid the debt.

"Well, you can imagine how hard it was to settle down to arduous work at 2 pounds a week when I knew that I could earn as much in a day by smearing my face with a little paint, laying my cap on the ground, and sitting still. It was a long fight between my pride and the money, but the dollars won at last, and I threw up reporting and sat day after day in the corner which I had first chosen, inspiring pity by my ghastly face and filling my pockets with coppers. Only one man knew my secret. He was the keeper of a low den in which I used to lodge in Swandam Lane, where I could every morning emerge as a squalid beggar and in the evenings transform myself into a well-dressed man about town. This fellow, a Lascar, was well paid by me for his rooms, so that I knew that my secret was safe in his possession.

"Well, very soon I found that I was saving considerable sums of money. I do not mean that any beggar in the streets of London could earn 700 pounds a year—which is less than my average takings—but I had exceptional advantages in my power of making up, and also in a facility of repartee, which improved by practice and made me quite a recognised character in the City. All day a stream of pennies, varied by silver, poured in upon me, and it was a very bad day in which I failed to take 2 pounds.

"As I grew richer I grew more ambitious, took a house in the country, and eventually married, without anyone having a suspicion as to my real occupation. My dear wife knew that I had business in the City. She little knew what.

"Last Monday I had finished for the day and was dressing in my room above the opium den when I looked out of my window and saw, to my horror and astonishment, that my wife was standing in the street, with her eyes fixed full upon me. I gave a cry of surprise, threw up my arms to cover my face, and, rushing to my confidant, the Lascar, entreated him to prevent anyone from coming up to me. I heard her voice downstairs, but I knew that she could not ascend. Swiftly I threw off my clothes, pulled on those of a beggar, and put on my pigments and wig. Even a wife's eyes could not pierce so complete a disguise. But then it occurred to me that there might be a search in the room, and that the clothes might betray me. I threw open the window, reopening by my violence a small cut which I had inflicted upon myself in the bedroom that morning. Then I seized my coat, which was weighted by the coppers which I had just transferred to it from the leather bag in which I carried my takings. I hurled it out of the window, and it disappeared into the Thames. The other clothes would have followed, but at that moment there was a rush of constables up the stair, and a few minutes after I found, rather, I confess, to my relief, that instead of being identified as Mr Neville St Clair, I was arrested as his murderer.

"I do not know that there is anything else for me to explain. I was determined to preserve my disguise as long as possible, and hence my preference for a dirty face. Knowing that my wife would be terribly anxious, I slipped off my ring and confided it to the Lascar at a moment when no constable was watching me, together with a hurried scrawl, telling her that she had no cause to fear."

"That note only reached her yesterday," said Holmes.

"Good God! What a week she must have spent!"

"The police have watched this Lascar," said Inspector Bradstreet, "and I can quite understand that he might find it difficult to post a letter unobserved. Probably he handed it to some sailor customer of his, who forgot all about it for some days."

"That was it," said Holmes, nodding approvingly; "I have no doubt of it. But have you never been prosecuted for begging?"

"Many times; but what was a fine to me?"

"It must stop here, however," said Bradstreet. "If the police are to hush this thing up, there must be no more of Hugh Boone."

"I have sworn it by the most solemn oaths which a man can take."

"In that case I think that it is probable that no further steps may be taken. But if you are found again, then all must come out. I am sure, Mr Holmes, that we are very much indebted to you for having cleared the matter up. I wish I knew how you reach your results."

"I reached this one," said my friend, "by sitting upon five pillows and consuming an ounce of shag. I think, Watson, that if we drive to Baker Street we shall just be in time for breakfast."

THE OUTBURSTS OF EVERETT TRUE